Winter Rose

Ace Books by Patricia A. McKillip

THE FORGOTTEN BEASTS OF ELD
THE SORCERESS AND THE CYGNET
THE CYGNET AND THE FIREBIRD
THE BOOK OF ATRIX WOLFE
WINTER ROSE

PATRICIA A. McKILLIP

WINTER ROSE

An Ace Book
Published by The Berkley Publishing Group
200 Madison Avenue, New York, NY 10016

The Putnam Berkley World Wide Web site address is
http://www.berkley.com

Book design by Irving Perkins Associates

First Edition: July 1996

Library of Congress Cataloging-in-Publication Data

McKillip, Patricia A.
Winter rose / Patricia A. McKillip.—1st ed.
p. cm.
ISBN 0-441-00334-6
I. Title.
PS3563.C3812W56 1996
813'.54—dc20 95-39317
CIP

Printed in the United States of America

10 9 8 7 6 5 4 3 2 1

for us all

Winter Rose

One

They said later that he rode into the village on a horse the color of buttermilk, but I saw him walk out of the wood.

I was kneeling at the well; I had just lifted water to my lips. The well was one of the wood's secrets: a deep spring as clear as light, hidden under an overhang of dark stones down which the brier roses fall, white as snow, red as blood, all summer long. The vines hide the water unless you know to look. I found it one hot afternoon when I stopped to smell the roses. Beneath their sweet scent lay something shadowy, mysterious: the smell of earth, water, wet stone. I moved the cascading briers and looked down at my own reflection.

Corbet, he called himself to the villagers. But I saw him before he had any name at all.

My name is Rois, and I look nothing like a rose. The

water told me that. Water never lies. I look more like a blackbird, with my flighty black hair and eyes more amber than the blackbird's sunny yellow. My skin is not fit for fairy tales, since I liked to stand in light, with my eyes closed, my face turned upward toward the sun. That's how I saw him at first: as a fall of light, and then something shaping out of the light. So it seemed. I did not move; I let the water stream silently down my wrist. There was a blur of gold: his hair. And then I blinked, and saw his facc more clearly.

I must have made some noise then. Perhaps I shifted among the wild fern. Perhaps I sighed. He looked toward me, but there was too much light; I must have been a blur of shadow in his eyes.

Then he walked out of the light.

Of course I thought about him, at first the way you think about weather or time, something always at the edge of your mind. He didn't seem real to me, just something I dreamed on a hot summer day, as I swallowed water scented with roses and stone. I remembered his eyes, odd, heavy-lidded, the color, I thought then, of his hair. When I saw them a day or two later, I was surprised.

I gathered wild lilies and honeysuckle and bleeding heart, which my sister, Laurel, loved. I stayed in the wood for a long time, watching, but he had gone. The sky turned the color of a mourning dove's breast before I walked out of the trees. I remembered time, then. I was tired and ravenous, and I wished I had ridden to the wood. I wished I had worn shoes. But I had learned where to find wild ginger, and what tree bled a crust of honey out of a split in the wood, and where the blackberries would ripen. My father despaired of me; my sister wondered at me. But my despair was greater if I caged my wonder, like a wild bird. Some days I let it fly free, and followed it. On those days I found the honey, and the secret well, and the mandrake root.

My sister, Laurel, is quite beautiful. She has chestnut hair, and skin like ripened peaches, and great grey eyes that seem to see things that are not quite discernible to others. She doesn't really see that well; her world is simple and fully human. Her brows lift and pucker worriedly when she encounters ambiguities, or sometimes only me. Everyone in the village loves her; she is gentle and sweet-spoken. She was to marry the next spring.

That twilight, when I came home barefoot, my skirt full of flowers, her lover, Perrin, was there. Perrin looked at me askance, as always, and shook his head.

"Barefoot. And with rose petals in your hair. You look like something conceived under a mushroom."

I stuck a stem of honeysuckle in his hair, and one of bleeding heart into my father's. It slid forward to dangle in front of his nose, a chain of little hearts. We laughed. He pointed a stubby finger at me.

"It's time you stopped dancing among the ferns and put your shoes on, and learned a thing or two from your sister's practical ways." He drank his beer, the hearts still trembling over his nose. I nodded gravely.

"I know."

"You say that," he grumbled. "But you don't really listen." He pushed the flower stem behind his ear, and drank more beer.

"Because you don't really mean what you say." I dropped all my flowers in Laurel's lap, and went behind him to put my arms around his neck. "You love me as I am. Besides, when Laurel marries, who will care for you?"

He snorted, even as he patted my hands. "You can't even remember to close a door at night. What I think is that you should find someone to care for you, before you tumble in a pond and drown, or fall out of a tree."

"I haven't," I lied with some dignity, "climbed a tree for years."

Perrin made an outraged noise. "I saw you up a pear tree near the old Lynn ruins only last autumn."

"I was hungry. That hardly counts." I loosed my father, and reached for bread, being still hungry. He sighed. "At least sit down. Never mind about getting the bracken out of your hair, or washing your hands, or anything else remotely civilized. How will you ever find a husband?"

I sat. A face turned toward me out of light, and for just a moment I forgot to breathe. Then I swallowed bread, while Laurel, gathering flowers on her lap, said amiably,

"Perhaps she doesn't want one. Not everyone does." But her brows had twitched into that little, anxious pucker. I was silent, making resolutions, then discarding them all as useless.

"I want," I said shortly, "to do what I want to do."

We lived comfortably in the rambling, thatched farmhouse that had grown askew with age. Centuries of footsteps had worn shallow valleys into the flagstones; the floors had settled haphazardly into the earth; door frames tilted; ceilings sagged. Other things happen to old houses, that only I seemed to notice. Smells had woven into the wood, so that lavender or baking bread scented the air at unexpected moments. The windows at night sometimes reflected other fires, the shadows of other faces. Spiders wove webs in high, shadowed corners that grew more elaborate through the years, as if each generation inherited and added to an airy palace. I wondered sometimes if they would die out when we did, or leave their intricate houses if we left ours. But I doubted that I would ever know: My father, with his wheat, and apple orchards, and his barns and stables, only grew more prosperous, and my sister's marriage at least would provide him with heirs for his house and his spiders.

Perrin was looking at me with that dispassionate, speculative expression he got when he was trying to imagine who among the villagers might be enchanted by me. I couldn't think of anyone. They were a hardheaded lot, though they were beginning to come to me for the healing oils and teas I made from my gleanings in the wood. Even Perrin, with his easy ways, would have been exasperated by me. And I would never stay where I was not free; I would simply walk out the door and vanish, vows or no.

That frightened me now and then, filled me with urgent, unreasoning despair, as if I lacked something vital—an arm, an eye—but did not know what it was I lacked that other people had to make them fully human. But most of the time I did not care. It would be nice, I thought, to have a Perrin with that wayward jet hair to smooth, or those shoulders to shape beneath my hands.

But not this Perrin. Nor anyone that I had grown up with, even among those whose own restlessness had led them to seek their fortunes elsewhere.

Laurel rose to put the flowers into water. I nibbled this and that: a chicken wing, a spoonful of raisins and walnuts in a sweet sticky sauce that our cook, Beda, knew I loved. She loved the wild herbs and mushrooms, the ginger and rosehips I brought her. Everyone else had eaten, not waiting for me to come home. My father got out his pipe; Laurel put flowers in niches and corners; Perrin found Laurel's flute and blew softly into it, beginning an old ballad of lovers parted on earth and reunited in the grave. He had not gotten through a verse when Laurel said sharply, "Don't play that."

We all looked at her, astonished. Color fanned across her face; she turned abruptly, shifted a vase an inch.

Perrin said quickly, "I'm sorry, love."

"It's bad luck."

"It's only an old ballad," I said, still surprised at the tone in her voice. She was so rarely cross or abrupt. "We've all sung it a hundred times."

She was silent. Then she shivered slightly and turned to us again, her face softening into an apologetic smile. "I know. It just—I don't want to think of such unhappiness now." Perrin stretched out a hand, wordlessly; she came to him, took his hand in both of hers. "Play only happy songs," she commanded him. Her voice was light, but her smile had gone, until he spoke.

"I will play," he said gravely, " 'The Ballad of Pig's Trough Tavern.' "

She loosed him then, and rapped him on the head with an empty tankard. "You will not. Play 'The Mariner's Lay for His Lady,' or I will never love you again, and you can take back the ribbons, and the blown glass horse and all your poetry."

"Poetry!" our father and I exclaimed together, and Perrin turned red as a cock's wattle. But he was laughing, and so was Laurel, and then, that was all that mattered.

A day or two later, I learned his name.

I had put my boots on, braided my hair, and ridden to the village with our father and a wagon full of apple brandy, which he had aged in small oaken kegs. While he delivered it to the village inn, I took a pot to the smithy to be mended, and bought ribbons to weave around sacks of dried petals for Laurel to lay among her wedding linens. The village was a scattering of houses, the stolid inn, a sagging tavern, an apothecary, the smithy, a stable, a baker, a weaver, a chandlery, the mill, and a swath of green in the middle of it, where geese and the weaver's sheep and the innkeeper's cow wandered. When I went into the inn to retrieve my father, who above all loved his ale and his company together, I heard the smith's lazy-boned son Crispin say, "My grandfather remembers it all: how his father and grandfather fought, and the son killed his father, and a curse was laid on the family with his grandfather's dying breath."

It was a moment before anyone sorted this out. My father said, "Wait—"

"His grandson," Crispin nodded, "it would be." He had a beautiful smile, and a smooth easy voice that made you forget the time it wasted. He sipped his beer, then enlightened my father. "Corbet, his name is. Corbet Lynn. His father died, and he has come to claim his inheritance."

"That old wreck?" The innkeeper, Travers, shook his head, mopping a ring my father's beer had left. "The land must be worth a fortune, but where's he going to live? The hall is in ruins. Nothing but a broken husk of stone overgrown with vines. The wood is taking it back. Will he sell the land?"

"He told my father no. He intends to stay. He's out there now." His eyes found a skirt and long hair in the doorway, and he smiled; he didn't need to see a face, just the suggestion of shape caught him that way. "Rois."

My father turned vaguely toward me. But his attention lay elsewhere. "Corbet."

Crispin nodded. "Riding through the village on a horse as white as milk," he said liltingly. "Or buttermilk, at least. Pretty. She threw a shoe at the crossroads. So we got his story first."

"His father wasn't hanged?" the innkeeper asked.

"No. He vanished. No one searched very hard for him. My grandfather said Nial Lynn had it coming. Anyway, no one saw anything."

"Then how—"

"No one admitted to seeing or hearing anything. But somehow everyone knew who spilled the blood in Lynn Hall, and how the family was cursed."

"What was the curse?" I asked, as entranced as anyone by such passions in our quiet world, and equally as skeptical.

" 'May yours do to you what you have done to me.' That's what my grandfather remembers."

My father's brows were up; he was thanking himself, I could see, for his wisdom in having only daughters. "And did he?"

Crispin shrugged. "Kill his father? He didn't mention it. He has his grandfather's face. So mine said. But others may remember differently. He seemed cheerful enough, if he did."

My feet had begun to want out of their boots. "Father," I said, and he rose. Crispin smiled at me again, raised his beer.

I turned, walked into the hot noon light, and saw him, with his pale gold hair and light-filled eyes, riding his horse the color of buttermilk across the green grass, as if he were human as the rest of us, not something that had stepped out of light into time. I could not move; I could not breathe. And then, as if he read my thoughts, his eyes met mine. Pale green seemed to melt through me, and I thought: How could they be any other color?

"Rois," my father said, and his eyes loosed me, and I could move again.

Two

Summer nearly passed before I spoke to him. I heard his name, now and then, on a wayward breeze. He had hired several villagers, including the indolent Crispin, to help him pull the fallen roof and the weeds out of the shell of the old hall. Crispin, I thought, worked out of curiosity about the man cursed to murder and be murdered. As the foundations began to appear, he hired other villagers to mortar stone walls back together, and to begin to clear the overgrown fields. Sometimes I drifted through the trees in the deep wood behind the hall. I caught a glimpse of him high on the stone walls, guiding a roof beam dangling from ropes, or in a room with three walls, studying a fireplace that stood attached to nothing. I never saw him closely. The loose angles of his body, the rolled sleeves and open neck of his shirt, the way he wiped carelessly at the sweat on his face and shouted for water, did not suggest either a man under a curse or something that had made itself in the summer wood and walked into the human world.

But I had seen him before he had a face.

The curse, among those whose memories had outlived their teeth, became the subject of long and rambling argument on hot afternoons. Each variation, born in blood and fraught with danger, riveted our interest on the man putting his house back together, as if the inevitable hung over his head while he bent to his work, and we could only guess if he would be struck by lightning before he fell off his roof, or before Crispin dropped a hammer on his head.

"My mother met Shave Turl's old aunt outside the weaver's today," Perrin said, at the end of a breathless day when the air seemed so heavy and full of molten light, everyone sweated drops of gold instead of brine. Perrin had been harvesting his fields; he had straw in his hair and stubble on his chin. We sat outside, watching the twilight birds wheel in the trembling air, watching for lightning. Laurel, as usual those evenings, worked at something dainty, sewing lace on a pillow slip, or embroidering a handkerchief with Perrin's initials.

She raised her eyes at Perrin's voice. Our father grunted and drew on his pipe. "He's even got Shave working," he commented. "Shave hasn't worked three days in the year. His bones are too delicate. Some days they can't even lift him out of bed."

"His aunt said that Crispin's grandfather remembers the curse all wrong, and his head is full of sheep shearings."

My father grunted again, this time with more interest. "What does she remember, then? I suppose she was there in Lynn Hall, rocking beside the great hearth while the boy killed his father."

Perrin shrugged. "Who knows?"

"Everyone seems to."

"Go on," I said impatiently, my arms tightening around my knees. I sat on the grass with my skirt trailing over my knees, my bare feet. I could smell the sweet crushed grass around me. "What curse does she remember?"

"She says Nial Lynn said to his son with his dying breath, 'Sorrow and trouble and bitterness will hound you and yours and the children of yours until Lynn falls and rises again.'"

My father raised a brow. "He said all that in one breath?"

"What did he mean?" Laurel asked curiously. "Lynn falls and rises again. The house? The family?"

"Shave's aunt couldn't be precise about that."

"It's a convenient curse, with the house beginning to rise already." My father tapped his pipe against stone. I looked out over the darkening wood, and wished I were something wild that prowled at night. I would run through moonlight until I reached the hall, where the wild roses grew among the tame in the old rose garden. And then, from some secret place, I would see what he became when moonlight touched him.

I shifted restlessly. Laurel dropped a hand on my shoulder, said gently, "Can you find me lavender, or roses—something sweet to scent my wedding cloth until

I work on it?" She had sensed my impulses; I had already brought her so much lavender to dry that the whole house smelled of it.

I nodded wordlessly. Perrin sniffed at the air. "No rain, yet." He fretted to be done with the harvest. Then the world could drown around him. Such stillness seemed charged, dangerous: There should be snakes' tongues flickering dryly above the trees at least, and the low, distant mutterings of thunder.

Laurel leaned back. "It's too hot to sew. My needle sticks in my fingers, and I can't remember what I'm doing. I can barely remember your name, Pernel. Or is it Perekin?"

"Don't," Perrin breathed, his face averted in the dark. She laughed and put her hand on his arm. They were both growing odd, prone to uncertainties and superstitions about their love. I supposed they would be unbearable by the time they married. And then they would forget their doubts as easily as you forget rain that falls at midnight.

She took her hand away again, her laughter fading. "It's too hot . . ." Her voice sounded unfamiliar; if I were an animal, I would have pricked an ear. I couldn't see her; all our faces had grown dark. If I had been her flute, I would have played a minor tune. If I had been her, I would have made a restless movement in the hot, sweet night; I would have wanted to touch and not touch; I would have misplaced my name.

The next week unburied another curse.

Perrin had got his grain into the barn; he helped our father finish his hay-making before the rains came. Each evening the clouds on the horizon turned the color of bruises, or overripe plums; the air seemed to listen, as we did, for rain. But the rains did not come. Work in the fields, work at Lynn Hall, continued.

Laurel, who had not yet seen Corbet Lynn, brought home the next curse. She had gone into the village to buy dyed thread and bone buttons and more linen, of which she seemed to require extraordinary quantities. She came to supper laden with gossip.

"Leta Gett broke another bone and is bedridden again. I asked Beda to make her some soup." She passed me cold beef and salad; it was still too hot to eat hot food. Perrin and our father, drinking ale, both looked as if they had, some time that day, dunked their heads in it. Their eyes were red with weariness; their hair stuck up stiffly; they wore threadbare beards, which they rasped absently and often but would not shave off until the hay was in. We ate outside again, fat candles smoking around us to drive away the insects. "I thought you or I could take it to her tomorrow, Rois. You could bring her some wild-flowers." I made a noncommital noise, my mouth full of radish. Laurel touched my arm, and lowered her voice, which caught the men's attention. "And here's a bit of scandal—Crispin must get married."

I swallowed what felt like a whole radish. "Who?"

"Aleria Turl."

I sucked in breath, just like an old gossip. "Aleria—she's a child! And plain as a summer squash."

Perrin grinned. "She's not that young, and she's had her eye on Crispin since she was seven. Maybe that's why he's working so hard suddenly."

"He'll take the money and run," our father grunted. Perrin shook his head.

"I'll wager not. He's still here. If he were going to run, he'd have done it the moment she told him. And he can't argue it's not his—everyone knows Crispin was all she ever wanted. And everyone knows her. He'll stay."

"He'll run," my father said briefly.

"He's too lazy to run."

"He'll not make his own wedding."

"He will," Perrin insisted. "He won't leave the place he knows."

Laurel looked at me; I shook my head. I knew both of them and neither of them at all, it seemed. That Crispin would father a child with a girl with eyes like gooseberries and a mouth like a paper cut seemed inconceivable to me; that she might possess secrets and mysteries that caused him to veer wildly off his chosen course of doing as little as possible was something no one would have bet on. But there it was.

"A keg of your apple brandy to a cask of my beer," said Perrin, who grew hops, "that he'll stay to marry her."

"When?" I asked Laurel. She was smiling a little, ruefully, at the bet, or at Aleria.

"Summer's end," she said. "How long can she wait? And that's not all—I found another curse."

"They're growing," our father said, slapping himself, "as thick as gnats."

"What is it?" Perrin asked, chewing celery noisily. I leaned my face on my hands, staring at Laurel, wondering at all the imminent, invisible dooms hurtling across generations at someone who had not even been born before he was cursed, if he had ever been born at all.

"Leta remembered it," Laurel said. "She had drunk some port for the pain in her hip, and she cleaned out her attic, as Caryl Gett put it."

Perrin chuckled. "Go on. What did she find up there?"

"That Nial Lynn had cursed his son with his dying breath saying, 'You are the last of us and you will die the last: As many as you have, your children will never be your own.' "

We were silent; it seemed, oddly, more terrible than the other curses. Perrin broke the silence.

"If that's true, then who is in the wood rebuilding Lynn Hall?"

I turned to stare at him. But it was an idle question; he did not wait for an answer. He pushed himself up, sighing, and went to kiss Laurel.

"Thank you," he said. "I must be up at dawn."

"I know."

"Will you miss me?"

"Will you?"

I got up at that point, and wandered across the grass. I heard our father call Beda to come and clear the cloth. I stood looking across the half-mown fields to where, I knew, Lynn Hall would be bathed in moonlight, broken and not yet healed, still open to light and rain and anything that moved.

"Rois," Laurel called, and I turned reluctantly. A stray raindrop hit my mouth as I went in. A few more pattered on the steps, vanishing instantly on the warm stone. I looked up, but it was only a passing cloud, a reminder of what was to come.

I took the soup to Leta Gett the next day, wanting to hear more of what she remembered of the curse and Nial Lynn. Who told you? I wanted to ask. Were you there? Who was there, that saw the murder and told of the curse? What did Nial Lynn do to his son that drove his son to murder? And that made Nial so hated that everyone looked the other way while the murderer fled? And if everyone was looking the other way, who was there to see what happened and to hear the curse?

But Leta Gett was sound asleep. Her daughter, Caryl, took the soup and the wild lilies I brought for her. When I asked about the curse, she only shook her head and sighed.

"It was a long winter, and too many people had too little to do besides spin tales. Nial Lynn was murdered, his son vanished, but no one was there to hear Nial's final opinion, if he said anything at all about the matter." Then she smiled. "It's all we're doing again: tale-spinning. Rois, will you make my mother a tea against the pain? She can't keep drinking port."

I promised I would. It gave me a reason to go back into the wood, to look for camomile and lady's-slipper. I would bring back water from the secret well, I told myself, knowing that I would go there, not for Leta Gett's sake, but for the sake of memory. I would drink the sweet water and watch the light. . . .

I crossed the green and heard the flock outside the apothecary's door: ancient men and women sunning themselves on his benches while they waited for his potions. In the light their hair looked silver and white-gold, their skin softly flowing like velvet, or melting beeswax. The gnarled bones in their hands resembled the roots of trees. They sat close to one another, arguing intensely in their bird voices, not listening, just wanting to remember. They paused briefly, their eyes, smoky with age, putting a name to me, a place. And then, as I entered the apothecary's open door, they began to speak again. I stopped in the shadows to listen.

" ' . . . will die at the year, the hour and the moment I die, and so will all your heirs.' "

" ' . . . will hate as I have hated, and die as I have died, and your sons, and their sons . . . ' "

" ' . . . never speak your own name again, and no one will know you when you die, and even your gravestone will stand silent . . . ' "

" 'None of your name will raise this house again, nor will the fields grow for any of your name, for I bequeath all to the wood and that is my final will.' "

I felt hollow suddenly, as if I heard the dying man's voice among their voices. The apothecary, filling a cobalt jar, said lightly, "They've been like this for days; it's just something to do. Telling stories of the dead, to remind them that they are still alive. Did you want something, Rois?"

I shook my head, swallowing. "Just to hear them. Just an answer."

He paused, then corked his cobalt. "It's my guess Nial Lynn broke his neck falling down drunk, and his son was never even there. Will that do?"

I bequeath all to the wood . . .

He has his grandfather's face . . .

I straightened, pushing myself away from the wall.

"It will do," I said, "until the next."

He smiled, though I could not. "Send Mat Gris in here, will you? And I could use more mandrake, if you spot it."

"Yes," I said, remembering. "I know where it grows."

And that's where he found me early next morning: beside the wild raspberries and beneath the silver elm, digging up mandrake root in the shadow of Lynn Hall.

Three

Again I could not see his face; it seemed blurred with light. Then I realized that he stood with his back to the rising sun, and though light spilled everywhere around him, his face was in shadow. He squatted down beside me to see what I was pulling out of his land, and I could see him clearly.

His face, like everyone's, was burned brown by the sun; his hair, streaked with all shades of gold, fell loosely across his brow. His lashes were ivory. He regarded me curiously out of heavy-lidded eyes; their green, washed with light, seemed barely discernible, an unnamed color that existed only in that moment. His hands, reaching for what I held, were big, lean, muscular; hauling stones, uprooting trees for half the summer, had laid muscle like smooth stones under his skin. He looked older than Perrin, or maybe only his expressions were older.

"I've seen you," he said, "in the village." His voice was light, calm; his eyes said nothing more. He looked down at what he held. "Mandrake."

"It's for the apothecary," I said. I still crouched in the elm roots, staring at him. He seemed human enough; he met my stare and matched it, expressing nothing but mild curiosity, until I added impulsively, "They say you're cursed."

"Oh." He looked away then, smiling a little. "So I've heard."

"Well, which is it?"

"Which what?"

"Which curse? Which is true?"

He stood up then, studying the mandrake root in his hand. He did not answer my question. "What's this good for?"

"Sleep," I said. "Love." I rose, too, aware of the soft bracken under my feet, the cool, crumbled earth beneath, the scents our movements stirred into the air. "It's dangerous," I added. "I don't use it; the apothecary knows how."

"Is this what you do?" he asked. "Find things for the apothecary?"

"I find things," I said. "Herbs for cooking and for soothing oils, flowers to dry, roots and berries that may be useful, or may not be. I don't find things for anyone; I take what catches my eye, and then give them away or use them."

"Are you a witch?"

The question made my breath catch, it was so unexpected. Then I laughed. "No, of course not. I just love these woods."

He smiled too. "Yes. So do I. You know my name; I don't know yours."

"Rois Melior. My father has that farm just east of your land."

"Ah, yes." He looked down at the root he held. "Don't you have a sister—?"

"Laurel."

"Laurel Melior." He said her name softly to the mandrake root; I heard the letters lilt and glide as if he spoke an unfamiliar language. Then he put the root into my hand. He glanced toward a sound; again his eyes caught light, and I thought, surprised by what I already knew: *Light does not always reveal, light can conceal.* "What is your father's name?" he asked.

"Mathu."

"Perhaps I will come and visit. It would be neighborly."

"Yes," I said instantly. "My father loves company. But I warn you, we are all very curious about you. Especially me."

He looked at me, smiling the little, pleasant smile that said nothing. "Why you?"

"Because you live in these woods."

His expression did not change. *I saw you,* I wanted to cry then, *shaping out of light beside the secret well; you are not human, you are wood; you are the hidden underground river; you are nothing we know to name.*

"Not yet," he said. "But soon."

"Soon?"

"I barely have a roof on my house to live here." He turned his head again toward voices—a shout, a laugh; his workers were arriving.

"Here comes your house," I said, and his face opened then.

"I hope so," he said with feeling. "At least one room, a door, a fireplace, and a roof over it all that won't leak icicles above my head all winter."

"You don't act like a man cursed," I said baldly; he shrugged the curse away, more interested in his roof.

"That's in the past," he said a little shortly, and I added, apologetic,

"Tell me if you want me not to dig on your land."

"Oh, no," he said quickly, and found my eyes again. "If you love these woods, you will do no harm. Come as you want, take what you like. Perhaps you can give me advice when I begin to clear the gardens."

I nodded. He lifted a hand in farewell, and went to meet his workers; I heard him whistle to a mockingbird, and the bird's mocking answer.

"I spoke to him," I told Laurel breathlessly, later, as I piled roots and myrtle leaves and wild orchids on the table. She fingered the mandrake root curiously.

"Who?"

"Corbet Lynn."

"Is this him?"

"What?" She looked up, then dodged the orchid I threw at her. She was laughing.

"They look so strange, these roots . . . like little shrunken images. Did you ask him about the curse or were you polite?"

"Of course I asked him. And of course he did not answer." I moved around the table restively, frowning, seeing him as he wanted us to see him, then, confused, remembering what I knew he was. "I was rude. He wouldn't be likely to tell some stranger how his father died, or what compelled him to return here."

"No," Laurel said thoughtfully. "You're right."

"But maybe with enough of our father's brandy in him, he'll tell us something."

She gathered the orchids. "You're very curious about him."

"And who isn't?"

"What does he look like?"

I opened my mouth, then closed it again. Words wanted to come out of me, words I had never used for any man. *His hair,* I wanted to say. *Those eyes. That warm skin. His hands.* I could not speak. But I told her; she stared at me, wide-eyed, and breathed, "Rois, you're blushing."

I felt the heat in my face then; I looked away quickly, wondering at myself. "It's hot," I said shortly. Laurel, tactful as always, studied the orchids as if they might suddenly take wing. But a little smile came and went on her lips. I leaned against the table, suddenly helpless in the heat, confused as much as ever.

"It's nothing," I said finally. "I'm not used to strangers. Around here, there's so little new to look at."

Her brows went up, and then together. She said softly to the orchids, "I hope he is a kind man."

"I don't know. I didn't ask for kindness. Just to wander in his wood."

She lifted her eyes then, smiling again, but still with the faint, worried frown between her brows. "Did he mind?"

"No. He loves the wood too, he said. He said I could go where I wanted . . ." The frown was fading; I added, "He seems to want, above all, a roof over his head. He means to stay through winter. He means to stay."

I heard her loose a breath."Good," she said briskly. "Then we can get to know him better."

"The curses," I said slowly, "deal so much with hate. There seems nothing about him to hate. He just seems—like one of us. Come home. But from some strange, distant place."

"Some strange past . . ." She was, I realized then, every bit as curious as I. As who wouldn't be, in that place where the little that happened loomed so large we were still talking about it down the generations.

I did not see him again in the wood then, though I could have; I could have looked for rosehips in the tangled gardens, or burdock seeds. But I could not pretend, under those strange eyes, about what I had truly come to find. I could have watched him secretly; I was afraid those eyes would find me. How could I hide anywhere in his wood?

So I roamed the wild wood, far from the sound of axes and hammers and voices, and waited for him to come to us.

He did finally, in civilized fashion, riding down the road after supper one evening on his buttermilk mare, carrying a handful of roses that had not been stifled by vines in the old garden for Laurel and me, and a bottle of fine port from the inn for my father. He had not accounted for Perrin, but he gave him a handshake and a friendly smile, and sat with us on the stone porch, as we always did, watching the day slowly bloom into night.

That's how it always seemed to me: not the fading of a withered flower, but the opening of some dark, rich blossom, with unexpected hues and heady scents. I sat to one side of Laurel on the steps; Perrin sat between her and our father on the long bench. Corbet dropped onto the steps, near my father, his body turned a little, as mine was, so that he could see both us and the fading colors in the sky. In the twilight, his pale hair and loose white shirt were vaguely visible. The rest of us were hardly clearer. Our father was a scent of pipe smoke, a burly shape; Laurel was a wing of white, now and then, when she lifted her hand to brush away an insect, and the light cloth of her sleeve glided on air. Perrin was a voice, a faint scent of hay and sweat, for he had come as usual straight from the fields. I don't know what I was: a voice, a pair of eyes, watching that pale head turned toward me, toward Laurel, toward our father, toward the night.

Then our father called Beda, and she brought us fat beeswax candles, and cups and my father's brandy. Fire streaked the dark; moths flew toward the flames, dancing around them, compelled and doomed, until fire touched them and they dropped like autumn leaves.

Light and shadow slid randomly over our faces as we talked: now revealing one eye and concealing the other, now stroking clear a straight jawline, now hiding a smile or a little anxious frown. As the brandy passed, questions came more easily.

"So you are to be married," Corbet said, looking from Laurel to Perrin. His head turned; shadow masked his eyes, but his smile remained. "Next spring?"

"It does seem long," Laurel said, answering the question in his voice. "But Perrin and I have known each other all our lives, and there's no reason for haste. I want to savor the expectation."

"With every stitch in every fine sheet," I teased.

"Yes, and lace on every garment. Also, Perrin has been building a cottage for us behind his parents' house, so we'll have a place of our own."

"You live with them?" Corbet asked Perrin.

"They're getting on," Perrin said easily. "My father still milks—he loves his cows. But I take care of the fields and even some of the milking; his hands are getting stiff. My mother cooks; my older sister does everything else for them. So you see, there's not much privacy."

"I see."

"And the house will go to my sister, if she doesn't marry, though most of the farm will go to me. I'd as soon have a place of our own. I'll build onto it, as we have children. But building takes its time—you know that."

"Yes." Corbet swallowed apple brandy. "This is wonderful."

"It's my grandfather's secret, the making of it," our father said, and Laurel swiftly caught up the thread.

"Did they know each other? Your father and Corbet's grandfather?"

My father was silent a moment, his brows knit, either trying to remember or straining to be tactful. Corbet said lightly, "Everyone knows everyone, here."

"I think," our father said finally, "they did not get along."

We all laughed. Corbet, his head bowed so that his hair shone and his face slipped into shadow, said ruefully, "What a reputation the man had. Even his dog hated him, I've heard."

We were all silent then, questions trembling along the weave of fire and night between us: *Why was he so hated? Why did his son kill him? What was the curse? How did your father die? Who are you?*

"Why?" I asked finally, and his face turned to me, fire catching in his eyes.

He said slowly, "My father told me some things when I was almost too young to understand. He must have told my mother more; I never asked her. She was very beautiful and wealthy, and she married my father despite his cursed past. I have wanted all my life to come to this place."

"Why?" Laurel echoed softly. He turned to her, his eyes again in shadow.

"I don't know," he said simply. "Perhaps it is the land."

"Or perhaps the curse," I murmured; he heard, but did not look at me.

"Perhaps," he breathed. Then he smiled suddenly and sipped brandy. "But I am too busy to worry about tales, and if I am cursed, what can I do about it? Throw myself off my roof to avoid it?"

Our father chuckled. "There's the crux of the matter. What can you do? Wearing your grandfather's face, you've stirred up some very old memories. But those who remember have few teeth left, and their minds are full of old bracken and fallen leaves. By spring — unless you provide us with something as colorful as your father did — we'll have other things to bark at."

"Laurel's wedding," Corbet suggested.

"There's always something."

"Except," I said, "that we will always be secretly watching for that curse to befall you."

"Well," he sighed, "I hope it doesn't befall before I get the roof up."

He rose then, leaving us, I thought, no wiser than before. But as he said good night to Laurel, I saw his eyes again, and suddenly I no longer knew what time might bring: a wedding or a curse or even another season. The night flower had opened all around us, with its dark, elusive colors and rich scents, holding us in its ancient mysteries.

Four

Summer ended between one breath and another, it seemed. One morning the first golden leaves appeared among the green. Then a tree flamed into crimson. The fields were stubbled gold, morning mists hanging over them, burned away slowly by the sun. Hot, blue summer sky slowly turned the deeper blue of autumn, as if it reflected, from another country, cold northern lakes and storms that did not touch us yet. I found great cobwebs everywhere, hung like chandeliers with prisms of dew. I brought home nuts and apples and bright sprays of leaves for Laurel. I found elderberries and juniper berries for Beda, and every kind of mushroom, until she asked, as she did every year, if I was trying to poison them all and inherit the lot. But the distorted shapes and unexpected colors of mushrooms fascinated me; I prowled through shadows and under bracken looking for them. They were ancient, wild things. No two were ever alike, and they had no roots to tie them to one place; like curiosity, they wandered everywhere. So did I, that brief, rich season between summer heat and autumn rain, when the light took its shades of gold from the dying leaves.

Though my father continued his dour predictions, Crispin refused to vanish as his wedding day grew closer. I saw him now and then, mortaring stones into place at the hall, or pulling them raw from Corbet's fields. I saw Corbet many times from a distance. I could not keep away from the wood. I found blackberries hanging huge and sweet on the brambles, still tasting of the summer sun. Beda baked them into pies flavored with a nip of apple brandy. I gathered rosehips and the last of the roses to dry their petals from the garden behind the hall. Corbet waved to me from his rooftop, balanced on a beam. I watched him, breathless, but he did not fall. Leaves drifted down into the open rooms, and windblown seeds, preparing to reclaim what he had cleared. But he had his wish at least: Two rooms would be whole before the rains came. He could leave the inn and live in the hall his father had left fifty-two winters before.

Winter would trap him there, and we were his closest neighbors. I envisioned him riding his horse through the snow to find fire and human company, Laurel and me and our father's apple brandy. Laurel would be sewing lace onto a sleeve and thinking of Perrin; Perrin would be softly playing the flute, and I would . . .

What? The question perplexed me, and made me restless. Woodland creatures did not fare well in winter. I had to wear shoes, I was enclosed by walls. Laurel told me I was impossible in winter; I might as well hibernate bearlike in solitude until I could be human again. What would Corbet do, I wondered, deprived of light, with only the shadowy greens of juniper and yew to break a wilderness of white?

I found a perfect ring of mushrooms one afternoon, beside the hidden well. Of course I stepped into it; what else can you do? My feet were bare, dirty, and scratched from blackberry brambles; my pockets sagged with chestnuts. I wanted to see what there was to see within the ring, and what I saw then, walking toward me among the burning trees, seemed both the last thing and the one thing I expected.

He looked amazed, too; perhaps only at the sight of a grown woman standing barefoot in the middle of a ring of mushrooms. He spoke first; I couldn't find my voice.

"Where are you going?"

It was such a strange question that I could barely answer; I was not moving, he was.

"Corbet." My voice shook slightly. "You're not working."

"In a sense." He looked at me a moment longer, blinking. Then he turned, and pushed aside the dying roses to reveal the well. "I'm looking for water. The old spring is dry."

I caught my breath. Had he seen me, that midsummer afternoon, kneeling motionless beside the well, water spiralling down my wrist, as I watched him walk out of light? Or had he smelled water like an animal? I had lived all my life without finding it until the day I saw him. He glanced vaguely toward me, at the sound I made.

"This is too far from the house. But if it comes from that direction . . ."

"How did you find it?"

He looked straight at me then, his brows lifted slightly in surprise. He had seen me, I thought, dazed. He hadn't . . . His eyes dropped then to a line of stones that branched away from the well. Moss clung to them; they were damp from the water running silently beneath them. They wandered between tree roots toward the house, charting the flow for a little ways, and then the water ran deep and left no hint of itself above ground.

Corbet made a move to follow, then paused. His shirt was loose, stained with dirt and sweat; his skin glistened with sweat. He shifted the rose vines again, carelessly; a thorn left a red weal down his wrist. He knelt beside the well and thrust both hands into it, drawing water to his mouth, his face, his dusty hair, splashing until his wet shirt clung to him, and the thick rose vines slid over his back as if to draw him deeper into the well.

He pulled himself free and stood finally, wiping water from his eyes, running his fingers through his hair, pushing it back. He saw me staring at him, and smiled a little. Gold leaves drifted down around him. I felt blood beat suddenly in my throat. His eyes changed; something as subtle as a change of light slid over them, and they grew opaque. He moved, and then I did, taking half an aimless step; I could not remember why I had come there, or where I had wanted to go.

"Can you use it?" I asked awkwardly, and he looked a question. "The well?"

He shook his head. "Pity," he said. "It's very sweet. It tastes of roses."

"I know."

He smiled again, his eyes still secret, like the well, which, suddenly, was no longer there. "Yes," he said softly. "You would know. You are drawn to secrets." He turned. "I must get back to work."

I watched him until he disappeared into the constant, gentle fall of leaves. Then I looked down and saw that the ring I stood in was also disappearing beneath the golden leaves.

I stepped out of it and went to the well. I slid apart the dying roses, and watched my reflection for a long time, until the faint rings and ripples he had left broke against the stones and faded, and the water grew calm, only trembling slightly with the hidden spring that fed it.

I went home then, still feeling strange, as if I had stepped between two worlds, and had forgotten which I had come to and which I had left. I shook the chestnuts out of my pockets in the kitchen, then took one outside to peel and eat. I sat down on the steps, dropped shell slowly. The sun still hung high above the horizon; I saw Perrin and my father in a distant field, cutting the dry cornstalks down.

Laurel came out to join me. She stood on the porch a moment, silently, watching the men in the field. Then she sat down beside me, and gave a little sigh. She said, "They're so alike, those two."

"Maybe that's why you love him. Nothing needs to change."

She was silent again. I saw Corbet bent over the

well, gold leaves falling around him, roses clinging to him, stars of water catching light, spilling over him, falling back into deep water.

"I saw Corbet," I said, wanting his name in my mouth. "In the wood."

She made a noise of interest or disinterest; I couldn't tell which. She said at a tangent, "Crispin will invite him to the wedding."

I hadn't thought so far. "Will he go?"

"He should. He could lay a few rumors to rest. It would be neighborly, which his grandfather, apparently, was not."

I nodded. The entire village had been invited to the wedding, despite the reasons for it. It was autumn; we needed something merry and mindless before the world grew bleak. There were a number of bets, I heard, that wouldn't be settled until Crispin stood meekly beside Aleria and pledged her his lifelong devotion.

"Nobody," I commented, "is betting that the bride will run."

"Not everyone is as restless as you. Where would she run to, anyway, with a child coming?"

"She should run. How long will Crispin stay faithful to those gooseberry eyes?"

Laurel gave me a little push with her hand. "Rois. Are you jealous? Did you want him?"

I laughed, looking down at my bare, dirty feet. "I suppose I haven't much better to offer him."

"You do look like a wild thing . . ." She thought a moment, her arms clasped across her knees, her face resting on them as she studied me. "Rois," she said again, softly. "We'll make you into a rose for Aleria's wedding. There's that dusky rose dress of our mother's with the tiny mother-of-pearl buttons down the front. You must find some roses in the wood—"

"They're all but dead by now."

"Find them. I'll put them in your hair, which will be coiled into a crown on top of your head, instead of flying behind you catching gnats." She straightened suddenly, smiling. "You'll be beautiful—no one will recognize you."

I grumbled something. But what I thought was: Corbet. He would forget about the barefoot, dishevelled woman standing like a wild child in a ring of mushrooms. I would make his eyes change when he looked at me, and this time he would not turn away.

"I'll find roses," I said breathlessly. "Yes."

Two weeks later, we stood on the green among the villagers, listening to Crispin's sheepish vows and Aleria's firm ones, while trees burned all around us against a clear sky that held within it all the shadowy blues of winter. Gamblers exchanged wry glances as the brief ceremony ended; I wondered how many coins and kegs, tools and hunting dogs, had changed owners in that moment. The couple kissed, and other, private bets were made: How long would it be before he . . . before she . . . They parted, turned and smiled, Aleria's hand resting calmly on her small, mute future. We cheered, and the music began.

We ate roast pig and corn, salads and breads of all description; we drank ale and wine and apple cider. The bride cut a cake dense with apples and nuts, and so redolent of our father's brandy that you could fall over, Perrin said, just from the fumes. He looked handsome, in a white shirt Laurel had made for him, his dark hair neatly trimmed, his harvest stubble finally shaved. When we finished eating, he swung Laurel into the dancing. She wore autumn red, which brought out the light in her chestnut hair, and the smoke in her grey eyes. She laughed up at Perrin as she whirled, lithe and slender in his arms, and beside me, our father said wistfully, "Your mother and I danced like that once."

"Then you can do it again," I said, and pulled him among the dancers. He protested, but stayed. I watched over his shoulder, saw the eyes that watched me, surprised and curious and smiling, but none of them with that surprise, that smile. Corbet had come, but late, and I had caught only glimpses of him—a flash of light hair, an ivory shirt sleeve flowing in a gesture, a tankard upraised in his hand.

"You look like her, in that dress," our father told me shyly, unaccustomed to complimenting me. He added, as I stepped on his foot, "You don't dance like her."

"I haven't had her practice," I said amiably. I had a circlet of wild roses around my coiled hair, and my best grey kid shoes with buckles on my feet. It was only a matter of time before he saw me.

Then I saw him, dancing with the bride who, torn between smiling at him and watching her feet, finally gave up on her feet and watched his eyes. They talked as they danced; I watched them both, wondering what he said. The music ended; he loosed her. I kept a firm hold on my father, whose eye was wandering toward the ale.

"It's a young man's work," he complained, but my sister had done her work too well: The young men did not know what to make of me. My father's feet were younger than his head; they spun me into circles until I felt my hair begin to slide, and a rose fell past my shoulder to my feet.

I crushed it in a step. Then someone stopped us, and my father, laughing and panting, yielded me into Corbet's arms.

"You look lovely," he said lightly. "A Rois among dandelions." I smiled up at him, but his eyes were elsewhere, caught by something over my shoulder: the color of a skirt, or maybe the fiddler's bowing. He added, before I could speak, "It's a pleasant afternoon for a wedding. Everyone looks unfamiliar, especially Crispin. I'm used to seeing him working with his shirt off and his hair dangling to his nose."

"That's an unfamiliar sight itself," I said. "Crispin working." Then I saw Corbet with his wet shirt clinging to his body, the skin golden and muscular beneath, and I felt the quick blood beat in my fingers touching his shoulder, his bare hand. His eyes came back to me, as if he felt something pass between our hands. I did not know, until then, that you could disappear into someone's gaze, that bone and heart and breath could melt like shadow into light, until only light was left. "Corbet—" I did not know whose voice spoke, whose heart beat so violently, whose fingers shifted from his shoulder to the bare skin beneath his hair.

"He'll have a rough winter," Corbet said dispassionately. He slid away from me and arched our arms, for me to spin around myself. Then he pulled me back, holding me loosely, his eyes on my face, but seeing Crispin. "Winter, and a child coming. I told Aleria I would use him as often as I could; there are things that can be done as long as we're not working with snow falling on our heads."

I tripped on his foot, feeling disoriented and clumsy, falling so abruptly back into myself. "Corbet," I said again, bewildered, pleading for him to feel what I was trying to tell him.

"I'm sorry," he said.

"It was my fault—"

"No, mine. I haven't done this in a while." He spun me again beneath our arms; his eyes, when he brought me back, were expressionless. "There. That's better."

I drew breath, still feeling my heartbeat, feeling, for a moment, the well inside me, rising and trying to spill into my eyes. I was trembling, as if I had nearly fallen, though I was not sure from where or why. "It's kind of you to care," I said. His brow went up a little; I swallowed dryly. "About Crispin and Aleria."

"I'm trying to live beyond my grandfather's face." He smiled a little, tightly. "People see what they expect to see. Except for you. You simply see."

I was mute a moment, gazing at him. "But I am not sure," I said, "what it is I'm looking at."

He did not answer, but his smile remained, still tight, thin; I realized then that he saw me all too well. The fine lady with roses in her hair and buckles on her dancing shoes was not the truth; truth stood in a ring of mushrooms in the wood; truth drank from a secret well.

"You'll miss the wood," he said suddenly, "in winter."

"Won't you?"

"I don't know." His eyes left mine, to wander through the fiery leaves around us. "I'm told not to expect many more days like this."

"The rains will begin soon." I thought of the well again, but now, in memory, more leaves fell between us, making him difficult to see. "There's water for you," I added.

His eyes narrowed a little, turned darker. But he was only considering my suggestion. "Perhaps I could dig a pond . . . channel the underground stream into it."

"You'll destroy the well," I protested, amazed that he could not care. He shook his head.

"Maybe not. Anyway no one ever knew it was there. Except you."

"And you."

He smiled again; his eyes did something else, still looking at me. "There are other places in the wood," he said softly.

"Other places?"

"Doors. Thresholds. Places of passage. That little well is very pretty, but in this world it will not be missed. I will try to be careful, though, because you love it."

I stared at him. He spun me gracefully, more gracefully than any farmer's son. I whispered, "Who are you?"

His easy, open expression did not change. "I am Corbet Lynn," he said. "I have returned to claim my inheritance."

"Returned," I whispered, "from where?"

He did not answer. His eyes had moved beyond me, again dark, intent. Impulsively, I turned us both half a circle, to put myself where he had been, to see what he had seen.

My sister, Laurel, still dancing with Perrin, turned him as abruptly, and whirled away, her back to us. But not before I had seen her eyes.

The music ended. I let go of Corbet. I did not know if he left me before I left him. I heard my name called once or twice as I walked among the dancers, but it was not his voice, so I did not stay. No one noticed me at the edge of the crowd. Perhaps no one recognized me; people see what they expect to see. I crossed the green and went into the empty inn, and out the back door.

I began to run.

Five

A wind came up and snatched the roses from my hair, then pulled my hair loose as I ran. I did not care. I stopped an instant to throw off my shoes; they landed in a corncrib. I gathered my skirt above my knees and headed across a cornfield. The stalks had not been cut yet; they blew wildly around me, their yellow leaves like hands, reaching out to me. The sky was still cloudless, but its blue had darkened; twilight rode hard behind the wind.

I was running from my own thoughts as much as anything. I simply wanted to untangle myself from the web I had touched. A single, sticky, quivering strand of it was all I needed to warn me away. I did not want to think about people. I wanted the trees, the scents and colors, the shifting shadows of the wood, which spoke a language I understood. I wished I could simply disappear in it, live like a bird or a fox through the winter, and leave the things I had glimpsed to resolve themselves without me.

The trees were bending like great fans in the wood. Clouds of gold and red and brown sailed along the wind. I slowed as I reached the privacy of the trees. A woman running across the cornfield in her mother's best dress is subject to human speculation; in the wood, the trees did not care. I could wear anything, think nothing. I walked until my hard panting eased, and then I began to run again, knowing what I wanted.

As fast as I moved, dusk raced me there. Night's season had begun; the days took what light was left them. I saw a last tender brush of sun slowly fade on the thick fall of rose vines over the well. Even stripped of leaves and roses, they would hide water, their naked thorns guarding against any touch. I did not dare get too close to the vines; the wind rattled through them, shook them, sent them whipping erratically in the air. One caught my hair, another my skirt, until I tore free and moved upwind, and settled down into the dead leaves.

Leaves blew against me from all parts of the wood and clung; I did not care. I only wanted to sit there, at least until the wedding was over, and Laurel came back home and Corbet went elsewhere. I did not want to see them together; I did not want to think about what I had seen in their eyes. It had been an aberration of the moment, something broken that could be instantly mended. As it would be, before I went home.

The wood darkened; the winds poured from every direction, not wintry yet, still carrying scents of ripe apple, blackberry, warm earth. But they sang of storm and bare branches and cold, shrivelled days. They were the harvest winds; they came to carry away the dying, sweep the earth for the dead. I had never heard them so clearly before; they seemed to have their separate voices, each wind its separate shape. I huddled in the leaves beside the well, watching the world darken, the moon rise slowly above the trees, leaves flying like flocks of birds across it.

I began to see faces.

Moonlight streaked the winds; in the mingling of moon and leaf I saw things that were neither, riding the wild winds. Night-black horses moved fluidly above the ground, silver harness sparked a silver light. Faces as pale and beautiful and distant as the moon flowed past me, as beautiful as Corbet's face. I heard their voices, the heart-beat of hooves, indistinct in the fall and whirl of leaves, the tense, singing winds. I could not move; I could scarcely remember anymore if I were human, or something the wind would snatch up and carry away into the season's end. Then a wind more fierce than any other blew the rose vines apart so that I saw the moon floating on the trembling water.

A shadow detached itself from the wind, dipped its mouth to the water and drank. Harness rang with small bells. I lifted my eyes from spark to spark: light on a stirrup, a rein, light on a pale moonlit face chiselled of ivory and ice and night.

I heard words, a lilting question, laughter as light and delicate as blown petals. I understood nothing. I crouched, staring, trying to make myself small, invisible, trying to turn into wind. The rider's slender hand rose over me. Something fell, glittering gold, dropped into the leaves beside me. I did not move. The rose vines tangled together again, left no hint of water. The winds darkened, galloped past me, great dark steeds with streaming manes and tails, their eyes reflecting moonlight. The leaves flowed after them from the ground, from the trees, a dry river rushing into autumn.

I did not move for a long time. Leaves piled against me, and blew away in passing winds. Leaves hid a shining, then revealed it, then hid it again. I waited, feeling my heartbeat, thinking nothing because I did not know what to think; I did not know if there were words for what I thought. Leaf has no words, nor does dark. I tried to become both of them, while clouds hunted down the moon, and it escaped, and they caught it again.

I felt my bones finally, aching to move, insisting on their human shape. I reached out then, still without thinking. I brushed away leaves until I found what lay buried beneath them.

I could not see it well; cloud had captured the moon again. I stood up and slipped it into a pocket. I wore my mother's dress, I remembered vaguely. I had danced at a wedding, in the sunlight. Then I had run across the fields into night, and I had seen, I had been given . . .

I shivered and took the first step home.

At some point, walking across our father's fields, I moved back into time. I saw lights in the house. I had no idea how long I had been gone. Perhaps they thought I had slipped away with someone, and no one had wondered. Perhaps they had assumed the most likely: that I had gotten tired of the crowd, and had gone wandering in the wood. I would come home safely, as I always had . . . I walked slowly, wearily, following the path of the moon; it stopped above the farmhouse as I stepped onto the porch.

I saw my sister turning away from the fireplace as I opened the door. Her face looked flushed, troubled. She had worried her hair loose; it tumbled around her face, only one ivory clip holding a wilted yellow pansy over her ear. She stared at me; I heard Perrin, sitting in a chair, murmur something. Our father rose and stepped toward me. Someone else moved in the shadows, and I closed my eyes a moment, for I had left nothing behind when I had run: It was all here waiting for me.

Then I opened my eyes and looked at him. His eyes withheld expression. He stood silently, leaning against the stone mantelpiece, not far from where Laurel had been before she saw me.

She breathed, touching my tangled hair, my torn dress, a weal on my neck, "Oh, Rois . . ."

I saw her eyes redden. Perrin and my father said at once, explosively, "What happened?"

"Nothing happened," I said shortly. "I went for a walk in the wood."

"With who?"

"No one."

"You left the wedding and you didn't come back and you didn't come here," Laurel said. "You disappeared."

"I'm not good," I sighed, "at weddings. I'm sorry." I looked at our father and said again, helplessly, "I'm sorry."

"You've been alone all this time?" He stretched a hand toward me. "No one—troubled you?"

Nothing human, I thought. I shook my head wearily, his failed daughter, his fey child, who had left her shoes in a corncrib to go dancing with the night. "You know what I'm like." I dragged leaves, the last rose, out of my hair. "I didn't mean to worry you."

They were silent, gazing at me, sensing more, but I had no more to give them. Corbet moved, and my eyes went to him. I saw, in some timeless moment, the shifting shapes of human and inhuman in his face, as if he looked up at me from within the well and the water trembled constantly over him.

He moved abruptly; my eyes dropped. I did not look at Laurel, but I felt her gaze. I moved closer to her, found her hand, and touched it.

"I'm sorry," I whispered.

I heard her sigh. "Never mind. You're safe, at least." None of us were, I knew then. "You must be hungry. Come into the kitchen; I'll find you something."

The men shifted, Perrin rising, Corbet moving from the hearth, my father turning down a lamp. "I'll leave you, then," Corbet said. "Since all is well." There was effort in his lightness. He caught my eyes again, briefly, as he crossed the room. "I was worried," he added, and I knew that he knew I had run from him. "I stayed to help search for you, if you did not come back."

"You would know where to look," I said softly. I watched Perrin kiss Laurel, and follow Corbet out. Our father closed the door behind them. He looked at me a moment, bewildered, anxious, wondering, I guessed, where the elegant woman he had danced with had gone, and what changeling child had taken her place.

He came to me, patted my shoulder a little, awkwardly. "Are you sure — " he began gruffly.

"I'm all right," I said. "There's nothing to tell."

He turned away, darkening the house, leaving the matter to Laurel.

I had nothing to tell Laurel, either. I ate cold ham and bread, and listened to her tell me how worried they all had been, how kind Corbet had been to stay with them, since he knew places where I went and no one else knew where to begin to look. I chewed wearily, waiting for her to stop talking. She poured wine, and watched me drink it.

Then she said gently, "Don't fret. Everyone runs from such things now and then; it's only human. People gather, and drink, and dance, feelings begin to fly like trapped birds, things get spoken without words, music suggests things that simply can't be . . . Lovers suddenly wear too-familiar faces, and other faces promise other worlds. . . ."

I swallowed a dry lump of food. I couldn't look at her. I said finally, "Maybe that's all it was."

"I'm sure it was." She touched my hair, stroked a strand back from my face. I looked at her then. She smiled, making me smile, though my throat burned, and I could feel the slight, secret weight dragging at my skirt. She drank her wine, and added, "You'll never guess who caught the wedding bouquet."

"You?"

"Beda." Her smile deepened at my expression. "And Shave Turl caught the straw crown that Crispin threw. He wore it for the rest of the afternoon, and tried to dance with every woman who didn't need a cane. Crispin's brother, Salish, asked where you were, and so did Ley Gett, and Tamis Orley—they wanted to dance with you."

I said nothing; she might as well have offered me shadows to dance with, since that's all they would have seemed after I had danced in Corbet's eyes. She sighed slightly, and drank more wine. She seemed, despite her dishevelled hair and worried expression, to have grown even more beautiful: There was a look deep in her autumn eyes, as if she had sensed the storm in a cloudless sky and gathered her powers to head into it.

But, in that quiet kitchen, it seemed impossible to believe what I had glimpsed. She loved Perrin, Perrin loved her; she would never hurt him, or our father. I would dance with everyone at her wedding, and I would run from nothing. I made a sound suddenly, a rueful laugh, wondering if I would dance barefoot.

"My shoes . . ."

"Where did you leave them?"

"In Ley Gett's corncrib."

Laurel laughed. "He'll think they fell out of the sky."

She put the food away and lit candles. I trailed upstairs after her, feeling footsore and very tired, too tired, suddenly, for love or terror or even for dreams. I washed in a daze, and left my mother's dress lying like a wilted rose on the floor. I crawled into bed with my eyes closed.

A hand, pale and slender, reached into the numbing dark of the first moment of sleep, and dropped something that glittered gold in the moonlight as it fell toward me.

I sat up out of sleep before it finished falling. I pulled myself out of bed, knelt beside my mother's dress, and reached into the pocket. I could not see what I found there; the room was black, or else my eyes were still closed. I took it to bed with me, slid it under my pillow, and slept then, hidden in night, in leaves, without dreams.

In the morning, I found only a dried, crumbled leaf beneath my pillow.

Six

The rains began.

Hard, constant, they battered the fields, turned the roads to mud, crushed the gold leaves into the ground and turned them black. In the wood, the sodden trees and brambles bowed beneath the torrents. Leaves fell, clung limply to vines and wildflowers, slowly buried them beneath their sodden weight. Work in the fields, on Lynn Hall, stopped, though I heard him hammering inside, the time or two I ventured into the wood. I went to the well once; the rain-kissed water gave me nothing, not even my reflection. Another time, near evening, when the rains had grown gentle, drops flecking the air like tiny fireflies, I went to gather the last of the crab apples for Beda. So I told myself: I had to pass the ruined hall to reach the tree. Smoke came out of a chimney, smelling sweetly of birch and maple. Crispin had brought him a wagonload of seasoned wood. I did not see him.

Most of the time, I stayed in the house, sewing beside Laurel, or watching the rain. I had frightened myself in the wood: I did not know, anymore, what was true. If I had invented a world that none of us lived in, then the true world was Laurel's, predictable, dependable, with no secrets and no stray midnight gold that turned to leaf by morning. Corbet Lynn had not walked out of light, but had ridden a horse into the village; Laurel loved Perrin as always, and I had seen wild horses in the night winds only because I wanted them there. I made myself teas of camomile and vervain to soothe my thoughts, and watched Laurel move calmly through her world. She never paced, or pulled a window open to feel the rain, the wind; she never moved without grace or purpose. She never went barefoot.

So I wore shoes and braided my hair, and made lace for her wedding dress, as if I sewed time and promises into each airy loop and every inch of it bound Laurel more securely to her future. And then I began to notice how softly my father spoke around me, and how he walked as if I were recovering, as he and Perrin sometimes did, from a keg of apple brandy. The little, anxious frown seemed always in Laurel's eyes when she looked at me. I had thought she still fretted over my stormy ramblings, but gradually I realized that my shod feet bothered her more.

"What is it?" she asked one afternoon, when we both sat sewing in the grey light from the window. "You've grown so quiet."

"I'm trying to be like you," I said.

She stared at me, amazed. "Why?" she asked finally. But I could not tell her why without telling her all the ways we differed, without painting pictures out of wind. She added, when I did not answer, "Usually by now you've paced a path across the ceiling, and it takes you the rest of autumn to settle muttering into winter. Or else you just go out in any weather, and come back wet as a fish, with your hands full of whatever isn't dead. You used to love the rain."

"You used to worry about that," I said shortly. There seemed no pleasing anyone.

"Rois—"

"I'm just trying to be civilized."

"But I miss the way you were." I huffed a sigh, and she said quickly, "I mean, I miss you being happy. You are never happy, housebound. Why are you forcing yourself so?"

"I can't be wild all my life." I missed a loop with my hook, aimed for it, missed again. I let lace and hook fall into my lap finally, and leaned back. Across the room, the window framed white birch, a muddy field, distant trees, looking ragged with the last of their leaves. I saw smoke rising above the trees, and I looked down quickly. Laurel, watching the same smoke, did not.

She said slowly, "I wonder what he cooks, in there. Probably half-raw meat and burned bread."

"He might eat at the inn."

"He might eat here." She stood up suddenly, briskly. "Tonight. You go and invite him. I'll tell Beda."

"Tonight?"

She threw a quizzical glance at me. "He must eat. And our father and Perrin like his company. Maybe he'll tell us more about his past. Go on."

"But it's raining."

She laughed at me incredulously. So I put my lace aside and contemplated my shoes. I hesitated; Laurel looked away discreetly.

I decided to ride to the hall. It suited my state of mind, which, like my feet, seemed both agitated and constrained. What expression would be in his eyes when he looked at me? I wondered in terror as I sorted through them in memory: his polite lack of expression, his remote smile, the way he looked at me without seeing me, or worse, saw far too much. But riding my calm dark mare, I was armed and in disguise: shod, braided, cloaked and hooded in green wool against the rain. His first expression would be surprise.

I rode around the ruins and found a door near the smoking chimney. I heard no noise inside. I dismounted and knocked: still nothing. I stood listening, wondering if he slept, or had ridden to the village. Then he said behind me, "Rois."

I whirled, my heart hammering. He walked among the old rose trees, his hair wet, leaves clinging like hands to his grey cloak. His shoulders and boots and the hem of his cloak were dark with rain; it did not seem to bother him.

"How could you recognize me like this?" I demanded. He would only have seen the back of a hooded cloak, and a pair of boots, and he did not know my horse.

He shrugged slightly, his eyes saying little, neither surprised nor unsurprised. "How could I not?" he asked simply.

I did not pursue that. I didn't want to be even more confused. I gave him Laurel's message tonelessly, adding dourly, "She thinks you eat raw meat."

He smiled at that. He walked to the door then, and unlatched it. "Come in and see."

Surprised, I followed him.

He had roofed two rooms and had hung a tapestry between them, a glittering fall of gold and silver thread, so ancient the threads had worn through in places, making the design dreamlike, imprecise. Roses framed it, deeply red, like old blood. The marble flagstones had been cleaned of moss and weed and half a century of grass. Some stones had broken, but he had mortared and smoothed the cracks, and scrubbed the stones to the color of old ivory. A velvet couch and a needlework chair stood beside the marble fireplace. Both trailed threads, but the dark wood had been polished until light caught in all its graceful scrolls and turns. Great raw beams spanned the ceiling above our heads; the roof, I realized, would become the underpinnings of another floor, next spring. Now rain tapped on it, soft at first, then harder, with insistent fingers, the wood wanting its own back.

"I had those brought from where I used to live; they belonged to my mother." He lifted the tapestry and let me see: a bed of the same dark wood, the cloths and canopy so precisely spread and hung that they seemed frozen into place, as if no one really slept there.

I saw no dust or spiders anywhere, nor anything he might have picked up in the wood: no nuts, or bowl of apples, or bright spray of leaves. "You don't eat raw meat," I said. "You don't eat anything."

"I eat at the inn," he said absently.

"And tonight?"

He smiled again, pleased. "Yes. Of course. It was kind of you to come."

"Laurel asked me to."

I watched him pull the tapestry straight on its wooden loops. His hair was the exact gold of those pale gold threads; he seemed, for an instant, his head and arm uplifted, his shirt blending into the flickering threads, a part of the tapestry, just stepping free. I felt my throat close on words, on wonder. *Have you seen the winds hunt*? I wanted to ask him. *Have you ever seen something as bright and heavy as gold turn into leaf by daylight*? His face turned toward me then, as if he heard my thoughts; his eyes held mine.

Again I felt their green drain through me, as if that color had become my heart's blood. He said softly, before I could turn away, "What did you see when you ran in the wood that night?"

I had seen his face, pale and alien and beautiful as the moon. The winds rode over me again, dark, wild, their cloaks of golden leaves, their harness forged of moonlight. I swallowed; my voice barely sounded.

"Wind."

"What else?"

"Water."

"What else?"

"A leaf."

His eyes loosed me then; I turned away, feeling dazed. Then I cried sharply, "Nothing! I saw nothing! Why do you think I'm dressed like this?"

"All in green," he said softly, "on a black horse, to bid me come and eat with you." It sounded like an old song. He added lightly, "Tell your sister I will bring wine from the inn. What do you like?"

"Anything. Apple or blackberry. Laurel likes blackberry."

"Then I will bring both." He opened the door for me. It was still raining hard, but I forgot, passing him closely, so closely I heard his drawn breath, to pull my hood up. I rode across the muddy fields blinded by water, my braids sliding loose in the wet, so that when I came into our house, dripping water and tracking mud, my hair in my eyes, Laurel finally looked familiar again.

He came at twilight, riding his buttermilk horse. The rains fell everywhere from an iron-grey sky, silvery ribbons in the lamplight, a constant hollow sound beyond that, as if the world were slowly emptying in the dark. He brought sweet wines, one dark, one pale. We drank them with stew and salad and black bread, and then we drank more around the fire, my father's brandy passing with the wines, while Perrin talked about his harvest, and Laurel's lace inched down from her hook, and I sat in the shadows, watching how the shifting light in Corbet's hair flickered silver and gold like the threads in his tapestry.

Perrin stopped talking after a while, and began to

play softly on Laurel's flute. Laurel's hands stilled; she raised her eyes to Corbet's face.

"Where did you live," she asked, "before you came here?"

He seemed inclined to answer; there was little, in that winey warmth, worth hiding. "In the city. In other places. My mother could afford to live where she chose. Sometimes near the sea. She loved water; moving or still, it didn't matter."

" 'I loved my love by water,' " Perrin said, breaking off a note. He was getting drunk. " 'I loved my love by land. I loved my love by the green, green sea, and left her on the silver sand.' " Our father gave a ghostly snore. Perrin raised his flute again to play.

"Go on," Laurel said to Corbet. "Where did you live just before you came here? In the city?" He nodded, sipping brandy. "Is that where your father died?"

"No," he said, and nothing more. But his eyes, cool, still, waited for another question. Laurel asked it, leaning back, her face framed by her dark hair, by darker wood, her eyes holding his.

"How did he die?"

"No," he said smoothly. "You should ask, 'Then where did he die?' "

"Did you love him?" I asked abruptly, and his eyes flicked to me, surprised.

"Now that," he said, "is a very good question. It would lay to rest any number of curses. But it will cost you an answer."

"To what?"

"Any question I ask."

Perrin, grunting a laugh, blew a sharp note. Our father straightened, blinking. "What was the question?" he demanded sleepily. "I misheard."

"Nothing," Perrin said. "Laurel and Rois are playing a game."

"I wasn't," Laurel protested. "I'm being seriously rude. Corbet is changing it into a game."

Corbet smiled at her over his glass. "Truth is a simple place reached by many different roads. I will tell you, but you won't believe me. My father is still living, but for understandable reasons he never wants to return to Lynn Hall. He married late in life; my mother died young. I inherited her fortune, and with my father's blessing I came to repair the hall and the land. With his blessing. Not his curse."

We were silent. I glanced at Laurel; she didn't believe him, either. "You told Crispin your father was dead," I said.

"I did not. Crispin assumed he was dead, since I returned to claim Lynn Hall."

"You let us all assume," Laurel protested.

"I didn't intend to," he answered gently. "It's just that no one asked me. And I was too busy to listen to gossip."

"It's a truth," I said after a moment. "Are there different truths, the way there are different curses?" I could feel the dark sweet wine pulsing through me; I had drunk too much, and it made me reckless. His eyes changed as he looked from Laurel to me; they withheld answers, emotions, held only secrets. "Or," I continued, "is each curse a different truth?"

Laurel laughed. "Rois, you're making no sense! Ask something he can answer, so we can understand."

"Yes," he said to her, and my breath stopped; he had answered me. I drank more wine.

"You ask," I said to Laurel, dazed by too much truth, and suddenly afraid. I wanted to hide myself in shadows the way I had hidden myself in leaves that night. But he saw through the shadows into fear: A smile, distant and cold as a star, surfaced in his eyes.

Laurel saw the smile differently; an answering smile touched her lips. He was a challenge to her, a teasing puzzle, something to unravel in the winter evenings, as long as he spun his riddles out. She contemplated him a moment, while Perrin played softly beside her, then asked, "Did your grandfather really curse your father?"

"Oh, yes," he said, and I saw his fingers tighten a little on his glass.

"And you?" she persisted. "Are you cursed?"

He looked at her without answering, until her eyes widened slightly and dropped. Perrin had stopped playing; he waited, curious, for an answer.

"I am cursed," Corbet said, "with a leaky fireplace, mutton four times a week at the inn, a horse stabled in my woodshed, weeds to the horizon everywhere I look, autumn falling into all the roofless rooms of my house, and winter waiting to take up lodging after it."

"You could leave," Laurel said softly, her brows crooked. "Come back in spring. Why don't you?"

"I have chosen to stay."

Our father stirred from his nap again, probably listening for the silent flute. "Good," he exclaimed, having caught a word here and there in his dreams. "Mutton, four times a week, that's terrible. You must come and eat with us, as often as you like. Come for the company." His affable smile, fat and warm as our beeswax candles, flashed at me a moment, then back to Corbet. "For the company," he repeated. "The winter nights grow old and thin and threadbare very fast, when you're alone."

Corbet rose. "Thank you."

"I mean it—you tell him, Laurel. See to it he comes."

"I will," she said, laughing. "If only to plague him with more questions, until he tells us the simple truth."

"I have told you," he protested. But she did not listen to him. I listened, but I had heard nothing simple at all.

He bade us good night. I left Laurel and Perrin talking, and went to bed. Sometime in the night he stood in my dreams, watching me out of his secret eyes, and I woke, shaken, still feeling his gaze in the dark.

Seven

I went to Lynn Hall again a few days later. I walked, but I wore shoes to leave at his threshold so he would find no wet footprints on his marble flagstones. The early rains had stopped. I had seen him riding out of the wood toward the village, a distant figure but recognizable to me in that unerring way your eyes find the one face you love or hate in the midst of a crowd. Sun broke between the thunderheads. Sheets of water on the muddy fields mirrored light, blue sky, great billows of cloud whipped to an airy froth, burning and paling as the sun passed in and out of them. I smelled wet bark, earth, rotting apples. Sun glittered everywhere in the rain-flecked wood. I caught drops on my fingertips, drank them from bare branches. My shoes and the hem of my cloak were drenched by the time I reached the hall. I left them on the doorstep and drew up my damp skirt in one hand as I opened the door.

I was looking for his past.

Except for a few smoldering coals on the grate, the place looked as if time never crossed that threshold. Was that, I wondered, where his grandfather had died? Beside his skinflint fire in the dead of winter? I searched the floor for a dulled shadow of blood; all I saw were the faint patterns the lichens left. I shifted the tapestry aside so that light fell into the small bedchamber. A chest beside the bed held clothes; the washstand held its bowl and pitcher, a razor folded into a handle of horn, a silver mirror. The mirror gave me back my face. Some part of me had hoped to find his face reflected there. The razor nicked me when I opened it; I put my finger in my mouth, caught my blood. I opened the bed curtains, drew back the fine wool blankets; I could not find, even in those soft linens, the imprint of his body.

I searched more carefully. He had left no trace of himself, not a single gold hair, not a smudged thumbprint on the polished wood. Perhaps he was unnaturally tidy. Or perhaps he did not sleep there. Perhaps he did not sleep.

Doors, he had said to me at Crispin's wedding. *Thresholds. Places of passage.*

I had not asked him what he meant; he had not wondered that I knew. He had seen me watching him when he passed between worlds. I had not questioned him. I wondered suddenly, intensely, what I knew, what I had stolen into his house to find. A bed that by night was a pile of leaves, a tapestry that hung between worlds, a bowl that held no water, a mirror that reflected . . . What?

I felt something shake through me: a premonition, a

vision. But the mirror held no answers; it reflected only what I saw. I paced impatiently between the rooms, wanting to peel the masks of things away, find out what they hid. A razor, but no soap. A mirror, but no comb. Clothes, but no shoes. I straightened the bed, closed the razor, pulled the tapestry into place. I stood a moment, studying it. The ancient threads suggested faces, shapes, but only if you did not look straight at them. They vanished into formlessness, if you searched, like patterns in smoke.

Doors. Thresholds. Passages.

Unless he came and went through the chimney, I could see no hint of a life lived between worlds, only a life lived in an eccentric fashion for any world. Perhaps, I thought bemusedly, he slept in the woodshed, and kept his soap beside a stream.

Or he slept, as he ate, at the inn.

I left finally, having exhausted conjecture as well as his sparse evidence. Wind rattling through bare branches shook raindrops on my head. I lifted my face for more; it was as close as I could come to tasting wind. Halls and palaces drifted overhead, following the sun. Had he come from such an elusive kingdom? I wondered, and then: Why would he have left it?

Not for a ruined hall on land the wood had claimed. Not for any mortal maid; I was the first he saw, and he had not come for me.

I wandered to the well. Water has its moods, flowing or still; it can lure you like a lover, or look as bleak as a broken heart. I pushed the faded vines aside and dipped my hand into the water. Wind rippled it, and my splashing; it would not give me my reflection. But it tasted of those great dreaming clouds, and of the bright winds and broken pieces of blue sky its trembling waters caught.

It tasted of the last sun before winter.

When I passed the hall again, on its blind side, I saw smoke blowing from the chimney, and his mare standing at the door, big, dark-eyed, still, as if she had just taken shape from something else waiting at the door, or had appeared too quickly from some place far away. I saw her look at me. But Corbet did not come out, and I slipped quickly and quietly away before he thought of me and I saw his eyes again inside my head.

Laurel laughed at me when I returned, windblown and muddy; she would not have laughed if she knew where I had gone.

I went to the village the next day, to take old Leta Gett some teas for pain and sleeplessness. Her hip had mended, but it still ached; the cold weather fretted her bones, and brought small ailments, one after another, like passing storms. She was grateful for the tea. Caryl brewed us both a cup, and left us, grateful for a moment to herself. Leta Gett's face was a little withered moon, with restless black eyes, and soft ivory hair so fine it slid out of pins and braids. She loved to talk when she was not in too much pain. She rambled through memory as you would wander from room to room in an old house you once lived in, filling it with stories: This happened here, and this here. Maybe they did, maybe you only wished they had; wishes blur so easily into truth. So I said his name. I tossed it like a pebble into a pond, and watched the ripples.

She got confused quickly by the past, thinking of Corbet, and remembering his grandfather's face.

"I remember how the wild roses grew around that hall. Nobody cared for the gardens; he was too mean to keep a gardener, and he had no interest himself. He worked the men in his fields too hard; he never hired as many as he needed. So no one went back for a second season. He made his son work even when he was small. The boy grew up wild and shy, like an animal; he hardly spoke, in the village. Once I saw a bruise like a hand on his cheek. I asked him—we were both children then, and children think the world is their business. Who hit you? I asked. And he got angry—so angry." She shook her head a little, marvelling at the memory. "He said he had fallen off a ladder. I remember his eyes, that turned so dark when he was angry or frightened. And he was always one or the other, it seemed."

"Where was his mother?" I asked.

"Oh, she came from far away, and died young. I only saw her once. She didn't seem real to me. Not like us. You know how children see things. Too full of light or dark, things are. She seemed made of lace or wings, nothing real. Not bones and weary skin—nothing that could ever be old." She paused, her lips twitching, her eyes suddenly too bright. "Nothing that would ache at the turn of the wind, or lose sight of her feet because she's too stiff to bend."

I put my hand on her hand. *Lace,* her soft skin said to my fingers. *Wings*. "How did she die?"

"Who knows, in that house? I saw his eyes, though

—we all went to see her buried. He wouldn't cry. You could see sorrow everywhere in him; he trembled at every wind, every spoken word. But his eyes were fierce as bitter winter night, and he would let no one touch him."

"His father?" I said, thinking of someone with Corbet's face standing beside such a furious and grieving child. His eyes would have been cold, ice over a running stream of secrets.

"Oh, he wept," Leta said, surprising me. "In front of us all. With no sound. No movement. The tears ran down his face, and he did not even seem to know what they were. . . ."

I shivered suddenly. Corbet must have glimpsed, in his father's eyes, what a terrible, violent, loveless place the old hall had been. But why had he come back at all, I wondered, if he had money and all the freedom in the world? Land, he had said. For the land. But he could have land anywhere. This village, like the hall, echoed with past. He had come to change an echo. Or perhaps I was right: He was cursed to return to the place where he had been cursed.

Leta drank more tea. Her eyes were drooping; she yawned. She moved more easily, comfrey and willow bark soothing her joints. She held out her cup, for me to take it, I thought, but she wanted more tea. She had not finished with her memories.

"One night after she was buried, one long summer night, warm like summer never is now, and with more stars than ever you see now, we snuck out of our beds and met on the green, and went secretly to Lynn Hall."

"Who?" I asked quickly, greedy for different memories.

"Crispin's grandfather Halov, and Anis Turl, and the innkeeper's girl, who ran away to the city—Marin was her name. She had her eye on young Tearle Lynn."

"On Corbet's father?"

"Yes. She wanted money, that one; she wouldn't look at the farmers' sons. Later she married someone with a ship . . . I think that was her, who did."

"So you all snuck out of your beds and went to Lynn Hall."

"Well, you know how children are, about places they're forbidden to go. Especially where someone has died . . . I remember the scent of the roses. We could smell them on the sweet air long before we reached the hall. Roses and the smell of new-cut hay. So it must have been that time of the year, the golden side of summer. And there we all were, running barefoot through the fields, thinking of what window we would push our faces against, to see what happened there at night. The place was so big, there were so many windows, the thought of them lit up drew us fluttering across the fields like moths. Chandeliers, Marin promised us. And gold cups. And fireplaces as big as kitchens, guarded by stone lions. We were almost there before we realized it, because the hall was completely dark, and we were looking for lines and tiers of light.

"It was late, they had gone to bed. But Marin made us circle the hall; she pushed us and whispered, and made more promises, of velvet hangings, and wonderful things to eat, on porcelain dishes, left untasted on a table as long as the village green.

"Finally we saw one light, in a corner room closest to the wood. It was on the bottom floor. A kitchen, I guessed, or the housekeeper's room. She was a surly woman, that one. She'd say just what she needed to say in the village, one word at a time, as if her mouth was full of straight pins. She wore black, with a black hat that looked like bat wings. She never spoke to us. She nodded to everyone except the innkeeper. She said 'Good day' to him. But never with a smile. Where was I?"

"You saw one light."

"Oh, yes. So we crept to it, expecting her. We were trying not to giggle, or whisper, but we kept tripping on each other, or stepping on thorns with our bare feet. We kept waiting for her face to appear at the window. A long horse face, she had. Bony and colorless as wax. She left at summer's end without a word to anyone. We just stopped seeing her after that."

Leta fell silent then, gazing into her tea. The expression on her face, I guessed, was much as it had been that night so long ago. "What did you see?" I asked eagerly.

She drew breath, blinking, astonished still. "Two rooms," she said. "One had a hanging drawn aside across its entry. We could see a bedpost in the shadows. In the bigger room we saw a single candle, and Tearle's father sitting next to it, just staring at the empty hearth. The door to the hallway beyond that room was boarded shut. That's all they lived in. Those two rooms. The rest of the hall was closed off. He must have put the housekeeper in the stable . . . Rois, you've spilled your tea."

The cup had overturned; tea flowed onto the saucer and into my lap. I stood up, brushing myself, feeling moth wings, moth feet, fluttering and prickling all over my skin.

"Dear," Leta said sleepily.

"It's all right. I'm used to being wet." I took her cup, too, before it slid out of her hand. She looked at me out of round, perplexed eyes.

"So we never saw a chandelier, and Marin ran away to marry a shipowner. Don't you think that was strange, Rois? That great beautiful house, and all they ever saw were those two rooms. Don't you think that was strange?" She lay back, dropped her hand over her eyes. "That poor, poor boy," I heard her whisper before I left.

Eight

And so I went to Lynn Hall at night.

I could not rest, I could barely eat, thinking of Corbet living like his grandfather's ghost in those two rooms. Did he know? I wondered, then: How could he not know? Nothing in those coldly beautiful rooms spoke of past by daylight. Were they haunted only at night? I paced, waiting for night. Our father, watching me circle chairs and weave between rooms, lift a curtain to check the color of the dusk, turn away and lift another, asked bluntly, with some humor, and more hope.

"Are you watching for spring to come? Or Corbet Lynn?"

I turned to stare at him. Laurel said quickly, shaking a cloth over the table for supper, "Father, really. Do you churn your butter with your feet, too? She's always this way in autumn. Leave her alone." She laid napkins. "Corbet is coming tomorrow, not tonight."

I stared at her then. "How do you know?"

"I saw him," she said calmly.

"When?"

"In the village. You were with Leta Gett. He asked me if he could come tomorrow. How is Leta?"

I twitched at a curtain, looked for chimney smoke above the wood. The sky had turned darker than smoke; there were no stars. It had not yet begun to rain again. "She's frail," I said. "But still gossiping."

"That's as good as breathing," our father said heartily. He hated to hear of illnesses, weaknesses among us. Perrin tapped on the door then, and came in, smelling of wood smoke and sweet, rain-soaked air.

He kissed Laurel, and began talking about a cow that had stopped eating. I watched the sky darken, until it was time for supper, and then I listened to the sounds of eating around me—spoons scraping bowls, Laurel's soft swallows, Perrin's noisy chewing, our father clearing his throat after every bite, Beda's heavy tread and breathing and I wondered how I would ever get through the winter.

It was better, later, when we sat around the fire, and our father's snoring mingled with the flute. Perrin played and spoke intermittently. Both the music and his voice were gentle. He did not speak of cows, but of the light in Laurel's hair, and of their childhood memories: how he had first kissed her among the blackberries, how they had first quarrelled in the apple orchard, throwing rotting apples at each other. My eyes dropped; his voice, Laurel's soft laugh, wove in and out of the fire's rustling; now and then the flute sang a little, a distant sound, as if someone played it in another room, another time.

I felt a touch on my shoulder and opened my eyes. Perrin had gone, our father had gone, the fire had dwindled into a glowing shimmer on the hearth.

"Go to bed, Rois," Laurel said. "You're dreaming."

I nodded. But I was where I wanted to be now: in the dead of night, and I sat there listening until I heard everyone's sleeping breaths. Then, barefoot, I crept outside, and made my way by lantern light to Lynn Hall.

I kept the lantern covered under my cloak until I reached the wood. Then I loosed a thin light to show me what bramble lay under my next step, what tree loomed in my path. The sky was very dark, without stars or even an edge of silver cloud to show where the moon hid. The hall took me by surprise, a wall of stone rising out of the black in front of me. The place was soundless; I saw nothing, I heard nothing. I stepped through a crumbling doorway into a room with no ceiling but the sky. I could feel the moss and broken flagstone under my feet. I let my cloak fall open. Light circled me, revealed jagged walls, window panes of sky. I moved from room to room, smelling the fresh wet beams that so far held up only air. I walked down the length of the hall until I stood at the doorway that Leta Gett had seen. It still sealed the two rooms behind it from the rest of the house, but the wood was newly planed and solid, a wall to keep out winter.

I could go no farther. Yet I stood there, my lantern raised, listening for voices behind the door, feeling the empty dark at my back, seeing nothing but wood, hearing nothing, as if I were in some timeless pause between a breath taken, a breath loosed.

I lifted my hand and knocked.

The door did not so much open as dissolve in front of me. The rooms themselves—walls, ceilings, furniture—seemed as insubstantial as smoke behind Corbet, who stood looking at me, his eyes as expressionless as the moonless sky.

He held out a hand. "You left something of yours here. You came back to look for it." It lay in his palm: a drop of blood, bright and gleaming like a jewel. As I stared, his fingers closed over it. "It's mine, now."

I felt a sharp pang, as if his hand had closed around my heart. "Corbet," I breathed. "What are you? Are you your father's ghost?"

"No." Expression touched his eyes; I saw him shudder. "No. Come in."

"No."

"You will," he told me. "You will follow me. You keep trying to find your way past the world. You still see your reflection in water, you still feel the wind rushing past you, leaving you behind. You want to dissolve into light, ride the wild winds. I saw you, that night. You wanted to flow like moonlight out of your own body. You will follow me."

"What happened?" I asked, holding fast to sorrow like a blade in my hands. "What happened in those two rooms?"

"Human things." He shook his head. "It does not matter."

"It matters. You wear your grandfather's face. Are you your grandfather's ghost?"

He made a sound; I saw his face streaked suddenly with fingers of red, as if he had been struck. "No." He lifted a hand, gripped the misty stone. "Come in and I will tell you."

"No."

"It's what you came for," he reminded me.

"I know."

"You came for truth, but you are too afraid to touch it."

"I am afraid of you," I whispered.

"Don't be," he said. But his cold eyes said: *You should be.*

I took a step backward; he reached out, caught my shoulder. "Rois," he said. "Don't leave me here. Don't leave me. Don't."

"Rois."

I struggled to open my eyes, feeling black leaves sliding over them, and over my face, my body, as if I pushed through some dark wood before I could wake. Laurel stood over me, one hand on my shoulder, a candle in the other. Only a couple of smoldering flakes remained of the fire.

"Rois," Laurel said sleepily. "Go to bed. You'll be stiff as a chair by morning."

I stood up unsteadily, bewildered, wondering if this were just another dream. *Don't,* he had said. *Rois.* I followed Laurel's candle; a leaf still wet from the wood glowed briefly on the floor in its light, like a footprint from another world.

When I first saw him the next evening, there was nothing in his eyes that remembered a dream of an open door between us.

He had ridden through rain, the interminable season between gold leaves and snow. He spoke of the weather, of a stable for his horse that he wanted Crispin's help to build on the clear days left to us. He had brought wine from the inn; as Beda brought us glasses, he counted them and raised a brow.

"Where is Perrin?"

"In his barn with a sick cow," Laurel said. His eyes questioned her, and she added, "He may come later." She met his eyes a moment longer, then pulled out a chair noisily from the table. "Sit down."

Beda had made a chicken pie, fragrant with tarragon and so heavy that only our father did justice to it, plowing a broad furrow through it that would set him snoring in his chair by the hearth. I couldn't eat. I was too aware of the movements of Corbet's hands, the tones in his voice, the candlelight sliding along the folds of his loose shirt, touching his skin. I listened for the voice I had heard in my dream: the voice that had said my name.

"Rois," he said, and I started. He was smiling, but I could see no smile in his eyes, only the reflection of fire.

"What?"

"You're very quiet."

"It's the season," Laurel explained. "She broods when she can't go roaming in the wood."

"But you were out a day or two ago," he said, and added easily, taking my breath away, "You left something in my house."

"You went visiting?" Laurel said. "You didn't tell me."

"I went for a walk." I had to stop to clear my throat. I could not meet his eyes. "I stopped at the hall. You were not there."

Blood, I thought. I left a jewel of blood where I cut myself on the reflection you left in your bright razor.

"What did you leave there?" Laurel asked curiously. "A few mushrooms? Some late apples?"

"Rainwater and mud," our father suggested, with a chuckle, pleased, I could tell, at where my heart had drifted. He poured more wine into my cup, heady and dark as old blood. I sipped it, then raised my eyes finally to meet Corbet's.

"What did I leave there?" I asked him. My heart pounded badly, but the wine steadied my voice. "I brought nothing."

He smiled again, shifting a little away from the light. "Then I won't tell you," he said. "And perhaps you'll visit me again. I need company. And you must come with her," he added to Laurel. "You haven't seen what I've done with the house."

She laughed, hesitating, I could see; our father reached for his pipe. "Of course they'll go," he said. "Laurel has been making enough lace to trim a barn; she needs light before the winter. She's my practical daughter," he added fondly. "I forget how she works in this house to keep it tidy and comfortable: the chairs always where you expect them, and the cushions never frayed, the carpets straight—I don't know what I'll do without her, when Perrin takes her away from here." He glanced at me, teasing, but I didn't know what he would do, either; I never straightened a carpet.

"I suppose," I said doubtfully, "you could hire a maid. Or get married again."

"I suppose," he retorted, "you couldn't just learn to dust."

"There's Perrin's sister," Laurel suggested. "Or Beda."

"Me," Beda said, snorting as she removed what our father had left of the pie. "Marry in order to keep house for someone? Who's to pay me for that? Now look at your plates—I didn't bake this to feed to the pigs."

"I'll finish later," Laurel said dutifully. "With Perrin."

We had all shaped a few designs on our plates, even Corbet, who had been working. Beda grumbled off with the remains; we took our wine to the fire and our father lit his pipe.

"This is pleasant," he sighed, after a puff or two. And after another puff or two: "But I miss Perrin on the flute."

"I can play," Corbet said. "My mother taught me." He reached for it, despite Laurel's protests.

"No, you must answer questions; you can't talk with your mouth full of music."

"Let me play a little," he said, raising the silver to his lips. "And then I will answer every question."

He played a little. None of us moved, not even my father to lift his pipe. It was a song out of a forgotten kingdom, out of the deep, secret heart of the wood. It burned wild and sweet in my throat, in the back of my eyes. It lured and beckoned; it gave us glimpses of the land beyond the falling leaves, within the well. He blurred into tears and fire, a face of fire and shadow, a gleaming stroke of silver. I wanted to find that place where such music grew as freely as the roses grew here, the place where the winds began, the place the full moon saw within the wood.

Then I heard his voice within the dream: *Don't leave me here. Don't leave me. Don't.*

He stopped as abruptly as he had begun. His eyes sought Laurel; she stared at him, her face flushed, her eyes wide, startled, as if she had just seen him for the first time, stepping out of light.

I felt the fear and wild grief flood through me. I would never see that kingdom; that song was not for me. As if he sensed my thoughts, his eyes flicked to me. *Don't,* he said. *Rois.*

He lowered the flute. "That's the only song I know."

Our father moved finally, tapping his pipe, which had gone out. He seemed bemused, as if he had heard something, or seen something, but did not know what to call it, and was not certain that he liked it. "It takes you," he said, but did not say where.

"My mother taught it to me," Corbet said. He put the flute back on the shelf above his head.

"It was beautiful," Laurel whispered. "I've never heard anything so beautiful." She blinked, stirring out of her spellbound thoughts. She appealed to me. "Have you, Rois?"

I shook my head, mute, wishing desperately for Perrin. We needed Perrin's boots and clear thoughts and the big, easy lines of his body between Laurel and Corbet.

And, as if I had wished him into being, there he was, coming into the room, shedding rain everywhere as he swung off his cloak.

"Cow's fine," he said, smiling. His eyes went to Laurel; his smile deepened a little. "You look awry—all bright and unsteady, like a candle in a breeze. Have you been playing your game of questions with Corbet?"

"We've just been sitting," she said. There was a little silence; none of us mentioned Corbet's playing. She rose abruptly. "Beda has supper for you in the kitchen."

"Good. I'm hollow."

Corbet stood up. "I'll bid you good night, then."

"No, stay," Perrin said. "We'll join you soon."

"There's brandy," our father offered. Corbet shook his head.

"I've been chopping wood," he said to Perrin, and Perrin grunted.

"You could use an early night." He slipped his arm around Laurel as she passed him; she turned abruptly in his hold to face Corbet.

"Next time," she said, "I will have questions for you. You won't get away so easily." She did not smile; neither did he. He gave her a little nod. Her eyes loosed him; he turned to get his cloak.

"Next time," he said, promising nothing, and left.

Nine

I went to the village to talk to Crispin's grandfather.

He was a brawny old man who still liked to pound a horseshoe now and then. He spent one night a week at the tavern, drinking with Crispin's father, until, red-faced and shouting, they would stumble home, waking neighbors and dogs, and swearing bitterly that they could not abide one more moment under the same roof with each other. In the morning, Crispin's grandfather would wake tremulous and penitent, and Crispin's father would wake oblivious of everything that had been said, and Crispin's mother would be banging pots in the kitchen, furious with them both.

So gossip told it, but this was not one of Halov's penitent days. I found him in the barn, whistling cheerfully as he pitched the mire out of the cow stalls. He peered at me with surprise, his eyes misted with the bloom of age.

"Rois?" He heaved dung out the door. "Are you looking for Salish?"

Salish was Crispin's younger brother, who had, unlike Crispin, inherited his grandfather's energy. I supposed Halov had become used to young women wandering around the place looking for Salish.

"I'm looking for you," I said.

Perplexed, he leaned on the pitchfork a moment. "Ah?" he said vaguely. I glanced around for some place to sit, and hoisted myself onto the top rail of a stall. He might, I thought, be more inclined to ramble if he kept working. I was silent until, bemused, he shrugged himself off his pitchfork and made a few tentative swirls in the straw.

Then I said, "It's about Corbet Lynn. You knew his father."

His brow wrinkled. He sent a forkful of straw out the barn door with a sudden, energetic thrust. "And his grandfather. That buzzard. Crazy as a bed quilt."

"Is that why Tearle Lynn murdered his father?" I asked, groping. "Because he was crazy?"

He stopped to rub his eyebrow with a thumbnail, as he looked back at the past. Then he rumbled and spat with some emphasis. "From where we all stood, if he hadn't, his father would likely have murdered him." He got to work again. "The boy was wild, like a dog goes wild, with ill-use, out of desperation. Nial Lynn scared us all. He was cold as iron in an icehouse. When he lashed out, you never saw it coming. That's how he was with Tearle. He'd walk beside him with no expression on his face, barely looking at him, and the next thing you'd know, the boy was in the dirt with a bloody mouth, and no one seeing it could swear Nial had laid a hand on him."

Corbet, I thought, chilled, then remembered: It was his father Halov spoke of, not him. There was no wildness, no despair in his eyes. "Except," I whispered, "when I dream about you." Halov, moving to the next stall, did not hear. My hands gripped the railing tightly; my heartbeat seemed strong enough to shake me loose.

Don't leave me here, he had said in my dream. *Don't leave me. Don't.*

"Everyone seems to remember a different curse," I said to Halov's back. "How would anyone have heard the curses?"

As if, I thought, I knew where "here" was, and how I could travel there to free him.

Halov seemed not to hear me; he didn't answer. But his pitching slowed a little, then slowly stopped. He leaned on his fork, gazing out the open doors of the barn, across the fields, as if he too searched for a frail thread of smoke rising into the grey sky from within the trees.

" 'May yours do to you what you have done to me,' " he said.

"Did you see Tearle kill his father?"

"It was dead winter when he died," he said softly to the distant wood. "I was huddled by the hearth in a dozen quilts, trying to sweat a fever out of me. The snow was piled halfway to the eaves. I would have had to shovel my way to Lynn Hall, to have seen anything."

"Then how do you know the curse?"

"Somebody had been out there, to bring the news

back," he answered vaguely. "The ground was frozen solid, but luckily there was the family vault, so we didn't have to keep him around until spring. No one showed up wanting his body, so we put him in there next to his wife." He moved the pitchfork again, but absently. "The hall began to fall to the wood then. It seemed a place that would stand longer than the village itself. But flood waters seeped up from underground, vines cracked the stones and pried them loose, snow packed itself on the roof, found seams and cracks to melt into until the roof rotted and fell. That's how old houses go. But this went far too fast, as if the hall itself were cursed."

"Who—" I had to clear my throat. "Who found Nial Lynn's body? Who brought back the news?"

Halov thought, then shook his head, his vague gaze returning from the wood to my face. "I don't remember. It seemed somehow that everyone just knew." I slid down from the railing; his eyes brightened a little as he watched me. "It's a good thing to check into, before."

"Before what?"

"Before you fall in love with someone cursed."

"No one seems to have heard a curse," I said a trifle testily. "Though you all know a different one."

"Well, maybe we invented them all," he said placatingly. We both thought about that, and came to the same conclusion. "No. None of us would have laid a curse on Tearle Lynn. He was maddened with despair, but not wicked. Not mean. We pitied him."

"Somebody cursed him," I said hollowly, remembering his son's despair in my dream. A cold wind whipped into the barn and I shivered. Rain tapped lightly on the roof, wanting in.

"Find Salish," Halov suggested. "He'll give you a ride home."

But I did not have the good sense to be interested in Salish.

I walked home in the rain, taking the road, puzzling over what Halov had told me. Someone had heard Nial curse his son, some cruel, bitter fate that no villager would have wished on the boy. But who? Maybe Caryl Gett had been right: It was a winter's tale, spun on long, firelit evenings, each version flavored with a different kind of wine. No one would see Nial Lynn come back to refute it, and from the sound of things, if Nial Lynn had a dying breath to use, he would have cursed with it. I was so engrossed in my thoughts I almost didn't see the buttermilk mare. Something—a flick of color, the faint beat of the earth under my feet, or maybe my name in someone's thoughts—made me lift my eyes.

There he was, riding across our father's fields. And there she was, wearing her teal blue cloak, her hood down, her chestnut hair streaming in the wind, riding with him on her dappled horse to Lynn Hall.

Again I felt the wild, unreasoning sorrow, that I would never ride with him like that, my hair and my cloak weaving into the winds behind me. And then I remembered what doors he knew, what thresholds and passages, and my grief turned to fear that he would leave, and take Laurel with him, and I would never see either of them again.

I ran across the fields, fighting the wind, ignoring the cold rain that the massed grey clouds scattered now and then like handfuls of seed. The fields were furrows of mud and stubble; I could not move quickly. By the time I reached the wood, smoke rose again above Lynn Hall. I slowed, winded and aching, my hair tangled and wet, my feet so muddy I stopped to clean them in a puddle. I did not know what I would say to them when I knocked; I only wanted to see their faces.

I heard their laughter just before I knocked. There was a brief silence. And then another laugh, and the door swung wide to reveal me, lank-haired and muddy, from some cold world beyond them. I saw the surprise in their eyes. Laurel sat beside the fire, her cloak in a heap on the spotless marble floor. Corbet swung the door wider after a moment. His eyes changed; their expression baffled me.

"Rois," Laurel exclaimed. "I thought you were in the village."

"I was walking home; I saw you . . ."

"You're drenched. And barefoot." She rose abruptly, her brows twitching together in that familiar worried frown. "You look as if the wind had blown you here."

"I think it did," Corbet said. "Leave your cloak there and come to the fire."

I unpinned my sodden cloak and dropped it where I stood, speechless, feeling awkward now, the unexpected guest who is neither invited, nor dressed for the occasion, nor prepared by wit or charm or beauty to persuade anyone that she should be here and not elsewhere.

I joined Laurel by the fire. Corbet poured a glass of

wine the color of golden apples into a crystal glass that looked as thin as a thumbnail.

"I hoped you would join us," he said, handing it to me.

You did not have this fine crystal before, I wanted to say. Instead, I just drank, while Laurel sat again, ignoring her wine, looking the way she had when I blew in out of the dark after Crispin's wedding.

"I thought you were Crispin," Corbet said, picking the name out of my head. "He is coming to talk to me about building that stable so that I won't have to sleep with my horse all winter."

"That's why we couldn't wait for you," Laurel said. She touched my hand. "You look very strange. What were you doing in the village? Did you visit Leta?"

"No." I drank more wine. They waited, so I had to answer. "I went to talk to Crispin's grandfather."

"Halov," Laurel said, astonished. "Why?"

"Did you see anything of Crispin?" Corbet asked at the same time. I shook my head, not believing his tale about Crispin and the stable. It was only an excuse to come here alone with Laurel.

"I would think he's home with Aleria," I said finally, and forced myself to meet his eyes. "I went to talk to Halov about your grandfather."

Corbet was silent. He put his cup on the mantel a little abruptly; a sweet note sounded against the marble. "You did."

"What for?" Laurel asked, bewildered and innocent, thinking she sat secure on silk within four stone walls. But I saw the endless wood around her, reaching out to her, as it had reached out to engulf Lynn Hall. The expression in Corbet's eyes, an odd mingling of fear and hope, surprised me.

"I can't get the tale out of my mind," I said recklessly. "Corbet tells us nothing, and you think it's just a game. I have to piece it together until I know what happened—"

"But Rois, it's not your business," Laurel interrupted.

"I don't care."

"That's very rude."

"I don't care," I said again. "Can't you understand? This haunts me—and it harms no one. The harm was done generations ago—"

"Yes," Corbet said softly.

"And it still haunts the village. Leta Gett remembers. Two rooms, she said they lived in—your father and your grandfather—two rooms only, in this huge place. She said—"

"Yes," he said again. His hand slid away from his glass to grip the stone beneath it. His face seemed calm, but it was the color of the marble. "These two rooms. My father told me."

Laurel turned from me to stare at him. "What are you talking about?"

"Why?" I demanded. "Why did you do it this way? Choosing to live through the winter the way they lived—are you trying to bring one of those curses down on your head?"

"No—"

"Enough," Laurel said, rising. She spoke sweetly,

but decisively, and we were both quiet. "Rois, you are being absurd. And morbid. You should go home and make yourself a tea. You'll catch a fever anyway, the way you've been running wild. And Corbet, you should not encourage this."

"Why?" he asked her, but gently. "Don't you think I am curious, too? And the villagers would never talk to me the way they talk to her. The ones who know, the ones who watched, who remembered." Laurel opened her mouth, her eyes pleading; he took her hand suddenly, stopping her. "It's like being lost in the wood. Everything and nothing points the way toward home. Every path is tangled; neither sun nor moon shed any light on the matter. I can do no more than I can. I build two rooms that mirror the past. Did I know that when I built them? Or did I only recognize them when I felt myself finally secure from winter? I can only do the simple things. Rois sees all the tangled paths."

Laurel gazed at him, wordless. Her eyes dropped to their touching hands; she did nothing for a moment, simply studied them, as if she were looking for an answer, a path out of her own wood. Then she slipped her hand free and sighed. "I don't understand either one of you. But I suppose you will do what you must without advice from me. Rois always has." She lifted her hand, looked down at it again, and added softly, "I am not so sure I understand myself anymore." She raised her eyes to his face and smiled suddenly, a little, bittersweet smile that made my throat burn. I did not dare look at him.

There was a sudden knock at the door. "That will be Crispin," Corbet said, and went to open it.

Ten

They had a few bright, chilly days to build that stable. I heard their hammering echo across the fields as I wandered toward the autumn wood. There was not much left alive in the wood; things were withering, dying back, withdrawing beneath the ground to wait through the winter. Among great masses of dead leaves, tumblings of brown vines, hillocks of stark brambles picked clean of their berries by the birds, branches torn down by the fierce winds, abandoned nests swaying on leafless boughs, a rare color caught my eyes: the burning green of holly, or the strange flowers of the witch hazel, their thin yellow petals curling like clusters of wood shavings on stripped, bare branches. I picked a few for Laurel, and found some rosehips for my teas. I did not go near Lynn Hall. I drifted, I felt, in Corbet's tangled wood, where light did not reveal the truth, and every path led into shadow.

He had told me where I was lost, but he had not told me how to find my way out of the wood. My thoughts roamed as I roamed, through the tales I had been told, through memories of Corbet, his riddling eyes and unexpected pleas, emerging out of dreams or casual conversations, for me to untangle paths for both of us. But I was afraid of the wood in which he was lost, and he knew it. I did not want to think of it, which is why, I realized finally, I did not want to see him. He did not come to the house during those days; perhaps he did not dare see Laurel. Perhaps he thought if he hewed enough, hammered enough, he could drive the sound of her voice out of his mind, he could build a wall against her eyes. She did not see him either. She kept the house spotless and sat with Perrin every evening. Only occasionally did she linger at a window to gaze at the distant wood which, with all its bare trees, still hid Lynn Hall within its heart.

I could not stop thinking, though I avoided thoughts that led down the most dangerous paths. I chose an easier way. I went back to the villagers to find the needle in the haystack: who had been in the wood to find Nial Lynn's body, who had heard his dying words.

" 'Sorrow and trouble and bitterness will hound you and yours and the children of yours . . . ' " Shave Turl's ancient great-aunt Anis said as I poured her a cup of blackberry tea. She had yellow-white hair and softly crumpled skin that draped itself in graceful folds over her bones. She had raised six children and buried four more in her long life. She moved stiffly now, and recognized voices instead of faces, but she was not infirm, and she liked her tea hot, strong and richly laced with cream. I sat with her in her quiet house; Shave, who lived with her to keep her company, had felt a chill in his bones and went back to his bed after checking to see if anyone interesting had come in to visit his aunt. He seemed inclined to linger, but when I offered to make him a tea to cure his chill, he took himself and his bones away. "That boy," Anis said, breaking off in the middle of the curse. "They're too delicate, these days. It's like soil, I think; one planting saps energy from the next."

It was a kindly way of looking at Shave, who once stayed in bed for a week while he lost a toenail he had stubbed on a harrow. I poured my tea and tried to ignore my own restless feet fidgeting in their boots. Outside Anis' thick window panes the distorted sky hung low and dove's wing-grey; the intermittent rains felt icy, and the wind had a sharp, testy mutter to it.

I said, turning her back in time, "How could you remember that curse all these years?"

"How could I forget it?" she asked with a certain, skewed reasoning.

"Other people remember different curses."

"It's as they remember."

"Did you see Nial Lynn die?"

She sipped tea almost as pale as cream. Her eyes seemed the same cloudy pale; she saw faces, she said, as blurs of shadow, though things farther away became, like memory, more detailed.

"I had a houseful then, and it was winter. That meant water boiling for laundry in one pot, soup simmering in another, bread rising, children everywhere underfoot, the littlest trying to walk, and apt to fall in the fire or out the door in a moment." She sipped tea. "Not," she said calmly, "that I would have stepped in to rescue him if I had seen it. He came here, sometimes."

"Nial?" I asked, startled.

"No. Young Tearle. Some years after his mother died and we ran free as rabbits that summer night to spy on Lynn Hall. I married young and already had my hands full, with my own and others' children come to visit them. Tearle would walk in, just come in like a wild thing out of the cold at odd times. He never said much. He would just sit and watch the others running and shrieking and laughing, watch me sewing, or cooking, or trying to catch one of them to bathe. I'd look up and there he'd be, like a ghost in the shadows, watching the children. He was much older than they, but young enough still to miss what he'd never had. They'd say his name, but they never teased him or bothered him. I'd go back to work, and look up again, and he'd be gone." She paused; entranced, I did not even blink. The lines on her face rearranged themselves, her thin mouth all but disappearing before she spoke again. "Once or twice I'd see bruises on him. He wouldn't let me touch them; he would not admit they were there. Once he ate a piece of plum cake I handed him. He ate it so slowly, crumb by crumb, as if he marvelled at every taste. Once he reached out and caught the baby when she tripped over her feet. Once she came and put her face on his legs and went to sleep. He watched her, not moving, until she woke again.

"And then he came."

"Nial," I guessed, as fine seams and wrinkles knotted.

"He came in without knocking, bade me good morning with a smile, and walked to where Tearle sat in a corner. He put his hand down, as if to help the boy up off the floor, and then—I don't know—Tearle started to stand, and was sitting again, his eyes closed, his head rolling limp against the wall, as if he had fallen asleep. Nial spoke his name, not sharply, and he struggled up, looking dazed. He stumbled a little, walking past me. I didn't see a mark on him. But something happened. He left without speaking. He never came again."

She lifted her cup delicately with both hands and drank. Neither of us spoke. The wind shrieked suddenly under the eaves and she started as at a child's voice.

"I never saw him much after that; I only heard the tales of him running wild with the wildest of ours. And then Nial cursed him and died and he ran away."

"Who heard the curse?" I asked. "Who saw Nial murdered?"

She was silent again, gazing at the clouds in her tea, watching a face form in them. She blinked; it swirled away. "I don't know that anyone saw it. Til Travers brought the news, though. He was broad as an oak, and burly, a great bullock of a young man, who would walk through a blizzard and not feel it, and not lose his way. He had a bird's sense of direction. He had taken a sleigh with provisions from the inn for the hall, a standing order every twelve days. I knew because my Nysa liked to ride with him, and I always fretted in bad weather. But she had sent him off into the storm that day. They had a quarrel, and she was red-eyed and scowling, and watching for him to come back anyway.

"And he came. He had Nial Lynn slung on top of his provisions, covered with sacks and two inches of snow. Nysa saw the blood on the sacks and rushed out into the snow to Til. He said there was blood on the marble floor, and Tearle Lynn had disappeared. He said something else, and then the children were wailing and Nysa was crying again, and Nial was sliding out from under the sacks, so I sent him with Til to the apothecary, who would know what to do if there was any life left in him." She paused; her eyes, pale as they were, fixed on her cup, reminded me of ravens' eyes.

"Did Til hear the curse?"

"He didn't say." She blinked and sat back in her chair. "What he said was that Tearle Lynn had vanished—"

"Yes—"

"But his horse was in the stable and there were no tracks anywhere in the snow except Til's. They searched, later. The snow lay unbroken all around the hall, except for Til's sleigh. Tearle Lynn had turned himself into a bird and flown . . ."

I stared at her, bewildered. "Maybe," I said finally, "he ran away before the snow fell. Maybe Nial Lynn's heart gave out and he struck his head, falling. Maybe Tearle never killed him at all."

"We asked all those things," she said. "They

searched all over the house, the woods. They found no secrets, no hidden doors or passages. But no one could explain the bruises around Nial Lynn's throat, or the table on its side, or the wine bottle smashed against the far wall. Nial Lynn had been murdered, and Tearle Lynn had killed him and had run. But out of what door and down what road no one could say."

I was silent. My hands were clenched under the table; I could feel my nails trying to hold thoughts still, but they ripped loose anyway, clamored like a flock of frightened birds.

He had opened a door and fled down a tangled path into the wood . . .

His son could not find the way back.

I shuddered, hearing the true curse that Nial Lynn had laid upon his son: *I bequeath all to the wood.*

And the wood had taken all.

I finished my tea and stood up. Corbet built his walls and his stable, roofed his rooms, spoke of clearing fields and finding water, but he lived among us as if each action might make him human, as if each wish, spoken, might make itself true. But it was little more than his father had done, sitting in Anis' house, watching, pretending that he belonged in that safe world, among those laughing, squabbling children, that the opening door would not lead him back to the cold and empty shadow world that claimed him.

"I must go," I said to Anis, but where, I did not know. I kissed her cheek; she drew a deep breath as I straightened.

"I can smell the wind and wood on you," she said, "as if you lived in them."

I opened the door and glimpsed, in the wild wind and sky, perhaps in her words, the next turn of the tangled path we walked.

Eleven

I went back to the well.

It was the only door I knew, besides the boarded doorway in Lynn Hall, and I could not go there. I was afraid to find Corbet behind that door again, luring me in, warning me away, with his grandfather's eyes and his father's desperate voice. He was not in the hall when I crept past it at twilight; the makeshift stable, finished but lacking a door, was empty. The sight chilled me more deeply than the winds. He could have simply gone to the inn to eat. But I saw him sitting at our hearth, watching Laurel out of secret, firelit eyes, while Perrin spoke of cows and our father snored. Play, I wanted to beg Perrin. Don't play cows and fields and next year's planting. Make a flute of your bones and play the music of your heart.

I had not been home all day. They knew I had gone to the village; they would think, when I did not return for supper, that I had stayed to eat with someone. What they would think later I could not pause to wonder.

Above the wood, the twilight sky was a dusky lavender, fading into deep purples and the vibrant grey of storm clouds. The winds smelled of rain; they held an edge of winter cold. They pushed me here and there as I walked, jostling me like invisible horses; they seemed to spring from any direction. Night came swiftly, caught me before I reached the well. But I stumbled on, guided by the lowering shape of a lightning-split oak against a moment's scattering of stars, by a pattern of stones underfoot, a sudden glint of water, the dry rattling of rose vines in the wind.

I smelled wet stone, and an echo, a memory, of sun-warmed roses. I sank wearily down beside the little well. The leaves were sodden and crumbling; I could not bury myself in them, but I did not care. I wanted to be found. So I did what Corbet had done, that hot summer day. I pushed aside the rose vines with one arm and dipped my hand into the water and drank. The vines blew against me, snagged my hair and my cloak, until I could hardly move. I lifted water and drank, lifted water and drank, until I felt it run down my throat and breast, and the thorns wove into cloth and hair and skin, imprisoning me, but I did not care.

Then I heard the voices on the wind, and the silvery ring of tiny bells. The winds flooded through the bare trees; I heard one snap like a bone and fall. Vines whipped wildly around me, opening to reveal the well, and the stones, and the rose as red as blood that bloomed in the dark water, more beautiful than any living rose.

"Take it," a voice breathed into the wind. I freed my hand from the thorns and reached into the water. It pricked me as I lifted it out; I smelled its perfume, all the scents of the summer that had gone.

"I want him," I said to all the dark riders crowded around me, who had ridden down the wind. "I want him in this world."

Silvery laughter mingled with the bells. "No one ever wanted him. And so he came to us."

"I want him."

"Then you must hold fast to him, as fast as those thorns hold you, no matter what shape he takes, what face he shows. You must love him."

"I do."

Again I heard the laughter, sweet and mocking in the screaming winds. "You must be human to love."

"I am," I said, and the tiny bells rang madly amid the laughter.

"Then take him."

His face appeared in the water, like the rose, as beautiful and as cruel, smiling his faint, secret smile, his eyes glittering with moonlight and as cold. I felt my heart pound sickly, for I did not want what I saw. But I reached down to him through the water, deeper and deeper, for he eluded me; deeper, until I felt the cold dark well up around me, and I saw nothing.

When I woke, he was bending over me.

The light burned my eyes, though it was only the misty grey of an autumn morning. His eyes were no longer cold; his brows were drawn hard. I raised my hand to touch his face, which looked as colorless and bleak as the sky behind it. Then I winced, and felt, all over me, the burning roses of pain.

"She's awake," he said briefly to someone. Perrin answered.

"I'll lift her."

"She can't ride."

Perrin's trousers appeared beside Corbet's face. "I'd best go back and get her father's wagon," he said.

"I'll do it," Corbet said, and stood up; I lost his face. "And some blankets to lay her on. And I'll bring Laurel."

"Yes," Perrin said, and I would have sighed if the rose vines weren't growing up my back. Nothing had changed. I felt a tear slide down my cheek. Perrin's face appeared where Corbet's had been. He took off his wool cloak and folded it, and slipped it gently under my head.

"Easy, girl," he said soothingly, as if he were talking to his horse. "We'll have you home soon. Looks like you fell into the brier roses, wandering around in the dark. Your sister rode for me at dawn; she went into the village to ask around, and I came out to the hall. Corbet brought me here. He said you liked this place."

"Where's my rose?" I asked, remembering it suddenly. Even my lips felt swollen. Perrin looked blank.

"What's that?"

"Where's my red rose?"

His brows lifted worriedly. "There's nothing blooming now, Rois. You're feverish. Lie quiet now, try to rest."

But I made him help me sit until I could look around me. The stark, thick vines hid the well again; perhaps, I thought, if I parted them, I would see the rose floating just beneath the water. But I could barely move, and Perrin would have thought me crazed. Perhaps he already did. Perhaps, I thought dispassionately, I am.

I pick roses out of water. I talk to voices in the wind. I see ghosts walk out of light.

Corbet finally returned, driving the wagon as close as he could among the trees; Laurel leaped down before it stopped.

She said nothing when she saw me; I saw her face drain white as cream. She bent down, touched my cheek gently. Perrin lifted me; she walked beside him to the wagon, holding the edge of my cloak between her fingers, not knowing where to hold me. Corbet helped him lay me on the blankets in the wagon. By then I was crying silently, partly in pain, partly out of frustration, because I could not tell them why I had gone into the wood in the dark, why I had impaled myself on rose vines. Laurel spoke at me as if I were a demented child; Perrin whistled, determined to be cheerful, and Corbet, wearing his calm human face, was not about to offer inhuman explanations to anyone. I hated him then. His eyes, touching mine, gave me nothing.

My father, horrified and speechless, helped them carry me up to bed. They left me there with Laurel and Beda, who drew off my torn, bloody clothing, washed me with comfrey water, and smoothed one of my own oils over my skin until it felt a little less like shredded paper and I smelled like a garden run wild. I was still crying; I refused to answer any of Laurel's questions. She gave up talking, and left me with a cup of camomile tea, which was, I found when I lifted it shakily to my lips, mostly apple brandy.

I slept without dreaming, except once, when a red rose opened in the dark and I smelled its scent.

When I woke, Laurel was lighting a lamp in a corner of the room so that I would not wake in the dark.

I said her name. She turned swiftly, bringing the lamp, and examined my torn wrists, my face. Then she sat on the bed and stared at me.

"Rois Melior, what on earth were you doing?"

I spoke cautiously; a thorn had caught my upper lip. "Nothing. It got dark sooner than I expected. That's—"

"Anis Turl said you came and asked her questions about Nial Lynn's death, about his son, about the curse on Lynn Hall. And then you forgot to come home before dark, you stayed out all night, and Corbet and Perrin found you in the wood near Lynn Hall, half-hidden in brambles, so tightly covered they didn't know at first if you were alive or dead. Perrin said it looked as if you were trying to drown yourself in thorns."

"I wasn't," I said shortly. "It was very windy—I got tangled, and the harder I pulled, the more tangled I got—"

"You stayed in the wood to spy on Corbet. What you're tangled in is that old moldering tale, which is nothing but memory now, in the few minds left to remember, and they don't know the difference anymore between what was true and what was conjecture, and what was just stories tossed around the hearth or the tavern after too much ale. That tale about the boy murdering his father and running away without leaving a track in the snow—there's nothing magical about it! Either he did or he didn't, and if he did, by Anis' account there was enough snow falling to bury the tracks of a harrow pulled by a dozen oxen. And I don't know what confused ideas you have about Corbet—" Color flushed through her face at his name; she continued determinedly, "But you must stop playing among his ghosts—it's stupid and dangerous and completely pointless. He's trying to lay them to rest here, not stir them up, and you seem eager to drag out all the sad old bones of his history and make them dance again. It's not nice and it's not fair."

I didn't bother pointing out that she, along with most of the village, had been just as curious. Perhaps the tale I was unearthing had shed its colorful drama to reveal a misery and dreary cruelty we all lived too close to. I stirred restively, then changed my mind about moving. My head ached; I wanted Laurel's soothing hands, not her anger.

"What does Corbet say?" I asked. "Does he complain about me?"

"Of course not. He doesn't complain about anything. But—"

"What did he say about finding me in the rose vines?"

"Nothing." But there was something; I saw it in her eyes.

"What did he say?"

"I don't know. He was with Perrin. He—" She brushed the air with her hand, making nothing out of something. But she liked to say Corbet's name, and so she answered. "Perrin said the vines were so thick they had trouble freeing you. He wanted to ride back and get pruning shears, but Corbet did not want him to cut the vines. It's a small thing, but Perrin thought it odd. He went back for work gloves, and brought the shears anyway, but by the time he reached the wood, Corbet had gotten you loose. He was bleeding, but he didn't seem to notice. I put your oil on his hands when he came to get me."

I turned my face away from the light, feeling tears burn down my face again. Had he, I wondered, opened the vines to see the rose floating in the water? Had he been there among those dark riders to hear my plea?

Had he laughed with them?

"Rois." Laurel touched my face with lavender-scented linen. The whole house smelled of me, I thought; I had brought the wood in here. "Don't cry. Just promise me—just try—try not to be so wild." I heard her take a breath. "If you think you are in love with Corbet, and you want him to take an interest in you, then you must see that with all the work he plans to do, he will need someone with a little common sense. Not a wild woman who roams the wood and flings herself impulsively into rose vines."

I looked at her. "But that's what I am," I said. "He knows it. He always knew. I can't hide anything from him."

She was silent, her eyes lowered, the little frown puckering her brows. She couldn't hide anything from him either. She reached for the jar of oil beside the bed.

"Turn over," she said. "And I'll do your back. Rois, you even have scratches in your hair . . ."

"I know."

"What did you expect to find, watching Corbet's life at night? That he eats and sleeps like the rest of us? That he might have a lover?"

"He might have twelve," I said, with my mouth full of sheet I bit when the oil touched my mangled skin. I felt her hands pause, questioning: *Does he*? *Who*? "But not from our village," I added, "or we would all know the morning after."

She made a light sound, almost a laugh; her hands moved again. "I am willing to admit that we've all been curious about him. But you seem possessed. Talking to Anis and to Halov—"

"And to Leta Gett."

"All to find out which curse he is under—nobody was there to hear one, it's just one of those tavern stories."

"Maybe." She drew the sheets down from my legs; the chilly air prickled over me. She wanted me to tell her; she wanted to hear anything at all about Corbet. "It's a sad story," I said temperately, avoiding what she would not listen to. "Nial Lynn was very cruel. He hurt his son in so many ways, until Tearle grew wild—"

"That was Corbet's father?"

"Is." Her hands paused again. "If what Corbet told us is true, and his father is still alive."

"Why wouldn't it be true?" she asked, but without conviction. I didn't bother to answer. She was silent a moment, weighing, I thought, her good sense against her curiosity. "Is that why Tearle Lynn killed Nial?"

"That's what they say."

"And then he walked on snow without leaving a track to follow."

"It must be as you said—" I bit the sheet again, as her fingers worked behind my knees. "The snow covered his footsteps."

"And no one ever heard of him again. He doesn't answer questions, does he?"

"Corbet?"

"Yes."

"You ask them," I said. "He may answer you."

She was silent again. I heard Perrin playing the flute below, softly, a lilting ballad of betrayed love. Music has its messages, but even I could not guess what misgivings lay behind Perrin's clear eyes. Perhaps none; perhaps he trusted Laurel without question. Perhaps he was right. All I knew is what Laurel's hands said when she spoke Corbet's name. And how often she said it, until it seemed, like the falling autumn leaves, or the long ribbons of migrating birds, one of the season's changes.

I stirred again, the headache raging behind my eyes, seeing Corbet's face in the well, his hand lifted out of the water, not to my waiting hand to pull himself out, but to catch Laurel's hand and drag her down.

"Is he down there?" I asked, sharply.

She did not even ask who I meant. She pulled the quilts up over me, and handed me the oil. "You can finish. I'll bring you some supper. He came to ask about you." I felt her hand on my cheek. "Don't think about him. Just try to be peaceful. Don't you have a tea for that?"

"Not for Corbet Lynn," I answered, but after she had gone.

Twelve

I dreamed of a red rose blooming in the snow. Corbet picked it and gave it to me. When I woke, I heard his voice, mingled with the sounds of Perrin playing the flute, Laurel's voice. I had slept through another day. Or perhaps there were no more days; they had withered and died for the season, left us with the winter flowers of darkness and dreams. I got out of bed, wrapped a quilt around me, and followed his voice down.

Fire bloomed in the dark, like the winter rose. I saw his face beside it. He smiled at me, shadow softly stroking his face, light catching in his hair, in a fold of his sleeve, sliding between his fingers. Perrin, softly playing on the other side of the fire, seemed to belong to another world; so did Laurel beside him, and our father falling asleep over his pipe. I went to Corbet; his eyes drew me, at once clear and secret, like the water in the well. He lifted a hand as I drew close, to draw me closer or to stop me. I took his hand and leaned over him. I felt the flush of fire in his skin, heard his indrawn breath just before I kissed him.

I heard the wind whispering around me, the trembling silver bells. Then the thorn bit my lip again, and I drew back.

That will cost you, his eyes said to me across the room.

I stood at the foot of the stairs, shivering despite the quilt, sweating despite the cold I felt deep in me. An unbearable silver fire glanced off the flute as Perrin lowered it. Laurel said, surprised,

"Rois. Are you awake or asleep?"

"I don't know," I said. I felt at my hair: a tangled bramble. I knew then that I was awake. Laurel rose quickly, felt my face.

"You're burning up."

"I know that. I want a silver cup."

"What?"

"To drink the rose floating in the well."

"You're dreaming," Laurel said. "There are no roses. Look." She drew back a curtain and I saw the first winter snow streaking the dark outside the window.

I looked at Corbet. "What will you do?" I asked, for the season of the curse was upon him. He did not answer; how could he know?

Laurel said, "He can borrow a lantern for the ride home. It's barely sticking to the ground."

Our father rose, awkward and perplexed in the face of illness. He came and patted my shoulder gently. I smelled ale and pipe and wood smoke, the smells of endless winter. "Should we send for the apothecary?" he asked me. I shook my head wearily.

"I have a tea for fevers."

"You spent a cold night bleeding on thorns," Perrin said grimly. "You might have caught your death. How much can you cure with those teas?"

I shrugged and was sorry. Corbet dragged at my eyes again, sitting silently beside the fire; I watched his face shape out of light, out of another world. Why would he want to stay in this one, winterbound in two cold rooms, waiting to be discovered by his grandfather?

"You should not have come here," I told him, and Laurel exclaimed,

"Rois, you're the one who shouldn't be here. Go back to bed. I'll bring you whatever you want. You must stop brooding over Corbet's relatives, or it will be the longest winter we have ever lived through." Turning, she appealed to him, holding his eyes. "Tell her what she wants to know, Corbet; she's possessed by your ghosts."

"She knows everything she needs to know," he said simply. "Except one thing."

"What?" we all asked at once, even my father, who, hazy as he was about the details, guessed there was some link between Corbet and his daughter flinging herself into brier roses.

"Why she needs to know."

Perrin grunted softly. Our father lifted a thumbnail to smooth his eyebrow, his face puckered. Laurel looked at me speculatively, her own eyes opaque for once, secret, and I shivered suddenly in fear, pulling at the quilt.

"I know why," I said sharply. He rose without answering; shadows slid across his face. He spoke to Laurel; his voice sounded strained, haunted by all the ghosts I had set loose.

"I'm sorry. It seems I can't help. I won't come again until you send for me."

"It's not your fault," Laurel protested as he took his cloak off the hook and swung it over his shoulders. He bade us good night; she followed him, trying to persuade him of several things at once, above all that he must feel welcome any time. Our father followed him with a lantern. I sat down on the bottom stair. Perrin lingered beside me, watching the snow swirling into the light about them as the door opened. I looked up at him. He met my eyes. Silently, we told each other what we saw.

He reached down, gently touched my shoulder. "You'd best get up to bed. This may well be the longest winter we've all lived through, and we'll need you strong."

I dreamed that night of Lynn Hall, as I had never seen it, perhaps as it had never been, with its fine, high walls the color of buttermilk, heavy silk curtains at every window looped back to reveal blazing clusters of crystal and candlelight, vast marble floors on which thin, bright carpets were placed as carefully as paintings, marble urns of roses everywhere. Entranced, I moved from window to window; each window I turned from darkened abruptly, as if such treasures only became visible when I looked at them. In the dark, I knew, the carpets turned to scattered leaves, and the curtains to spider web; rose petals the color of blood spilled onto the marble floors.

I heard his voice.

Don't leave me here.

Rois.

I woke to find smooth cold sky mirroring smooth cold fields. The world had turned as colorless and shadowless as the face of the moon, and as small; our horizons ringed us closely, reaching down, reaching up, to touch white. I wanted to bury myself away from the sight, under goose-down or leaves, until spring. I never knew what to do when the world turned skeletal and mute, with nothing but withered stalks pushing up between its bones.

Perversely, I felt better, weak but clear-headed, and in far less pain. I vaguely remembered the things I had said to Corbet. Even in such stark daylight they seemed urgent and true; the winter curse lay over him, and in his two sparse rooms he waited for it. Or in some cold world he waited for the wood to claim him, for his house would never be rebuilt, nor would his fields grow for him.

I bequeath all to the wood.

I got up restlessly, to look out the window and see which way the wind blew the smoke above Lynn Hall.

The wind had blown Corbet's way: I saw a set of fresh hoof prints in the snow, coming and going, or going and coming. I heard Laurel's steps on the stairs, as if she had heard mine overhead. Her face was still bright with cold; she carried Corbet in her eyes, the smile he had given her on her lips. She smelled of winter.

"Rois." She felt my face, then saw what I was looking at. She said composedly, "You look better. I rode over to invite him for supper. Father sent me. He seems to think Corbet's presence will keep you from brooding about his absence."

I did not say what I thought; perhaps, if it remained unspoken, it would become untrue. I said tiredly, "I will try to be civilized." My feet were cold. I got back into bed, wondering how I could find a door or passage out of this bleak world. Even the well would be covered with a sheen of ice. Perhaps Corbet would give me a key. And then I remembered what he had said: She knows everything she needs to know.

Except one thing.

Why.

I lay back, closed my eyes. I had no idea what he meant. *Why she needs to know* . . . And I did not care. Need is need; it is its own explanation. Laurel said something about soup. I made a noise; she disappeared again. I slept a little; a voice as sweet as silver bells, as secret as the wind said: *You must hold fast to him, as fast as those thorns hold you, no matter what shape he takes. . . .*

The door opened; I heard no step. "Laurel?" I said with my eyes closed. No one answered. The door closed softly. One of the house's memories, I thought in my sleep. The door opened again; Laurel said as she came in, "Father is riding to the village. Do you want anything? Rois . . ." Her voice trailed away. I opened my eyes.

The room smelled of roses, profuse and sun-warmed, on a hot midsummer day. Laurel, her thoughts drifting, seemed entranced but puzzled, as if she could not have said what caught her by surprise. She moved finally, set a tray of bread and soup on the bed. I said sleepily, "It's the house. Sometimes it does that."

"What?"

"Remembers a different smell."

"Rois, you're making no sense again. Here. Eat this."

"Suppose I am," I argued dourly. "Suppose I am the only one in this house making any sense at all. Suppose that everything I say is true, and everything I do is vital—"

"All right," she said. "I'll suppose. Corbet is cursed and you are trying—by some peculiar means—to rescue him. Now what?" I couldn't answer; I had no answers yet. She turned away; I saw her hands rise, push themselves briefly against her eyes. "Just be careful, Rois. Just don't get hurt."

I bathed myself for the first time in days, in water softened with oils of camomile and rose. I dressed, then combed my hair dry before the fire, thinking all the while of Corbet, wondering which way to turn next, what to do to help him, not knowing what to do to help any of us out of the trouble we headed into. Perrin did not appear for supper; another sick animal kept him home. Corbet came late. He brought wine with him, not from the inn, he said, but from some other place.

"What other place?" Laurel asked, smiling. "In winter, there are no other places."

He smiled back at her, but did not answer. He poured wine into three of the cups Beda brought, handed one to Laurel, one to our father. Our father tasted it. His brows went up; he became suddenly lyrical.

"It's wonderful—it tastes like the smell of new-mown hay." He took another sip. "In early morning, wet with dew."

"It does not taste like hay." Laurel laughed. "It tastes like the year's first sweet bite of peach, warm from the sun and so ripe it slides off the bough into your hand when you touch it."

Corbet raised the third cup to his lips. "Golden apples," he said. "And hazelnuts." He looked at me. "Rois—I forgot. I brought you what you asked for." He turned, while we watched, baffled. He reached into the pocket of his cloak and pulled out a silver cup.

I smiled a little, and then I saw his eyes: He was not humoring a sick child. Laurel exclaimed over the cup. Roses spiralled up its stem, spilled around its sides, trailed down over its lip. Our father beamed at Corbet, pleased with himself as well, for asking him to come. I stared at the cup as Corbet poured wine, feeling my heart beat in my throat. The wine, by candlelight, was of such pale gold it looked like water.

He handed me the cup. I smelled roses and wet stone. In the bottom of the cup, a reflection of flame from a candle in its sconce above my shoulder changed into a blood-red rose.

"Drink," he said. I looked into his eyes; they seemed colder and more distant than the stars.

I raised the cup to my lips and drank.

Thirteen

I saw the world out of Corbet's eyes.

Our solid walls crumbled, showed stone under broken plaster, and night where stone had fallen. Winds, dark and faceless, flew restlessly in and out of the holes in the roof between the sagging rafters. Beda and my father were shadowy figures, bulky, indistinct, their voices blurred, their gestures ragged and abrupt, like the gestures of scarecrows. The fire fluttered frantically in the darkness, giving little warmth and less light, even when the shadow with the burning pipe rose with a laugh that seemed to ripple across the air, echoing itself, and heaved a log into the flames. Only Laurel seemed unchanged, a glowing figure. Light caught at her and clung, framed her tranquil movements. Her voice came clearly through the errant winds, the constant flow of dry, invisible leaves rushing across flagstones, down all our crooked, meandering passageways.

I didn't see myself out of his eyes. But I saw his face, pale as moonlight, as if the sun had never touched it. Expressions shaped it with every touch of wind. Generations looked out of his eyes. Now he wore his grandfather's dangerous smile, now his father's helpless fury; now his own terror touched his eyes, or his desperate need for the one clear, bright figure in his world. And then he would look at me and his face would change again, beautiful and merciless, luring me and warning me away.

Wind pulled at my skirts as we sat at the table. Like him, I followed Laurel's calm lead and pulled out my chair, though one slat in the seat fell and scraped the flagstones as I sat. A faceless Beda, her cap like a frilly mushroom on her head, brought in something on a silver tray. Leaves, it seemed, or withered petals, flowed out of her ladle into our bowls. I watched Laurel numbly. She picked up her spoon and ate; so did our father, pulling dry, splintering wood apart to dip into his bowl.

"What is this?" I breathed to Corbet. "What is this place? Is this where you live?"

His eyes answered me. A sudden wind sang with an edged, dangerous voice; his face changed, grew taut, haunted.

"You're not eating," Laurel said in another world. "Rois. Corbet."

"Eat," our father urged. "It's Beda's finest: onion and potato soup. Rois, you have hardly touched a morsel in days."

I picked up my spoon; it was tarnished, and so worn the silver parted into strands like a web. "Is this the place where you will answer questions?"

He did not answer. His face changed again, as a figure came to stand behind his chair.

I knew that face, though I had never seen it so clearly before: that moonlight skin, those eyes the elusive burning blue of stars. Her midnight hair mingled with the winds, flowed everywhere, glittering as with stars.

She laid an impossibly pale and delicate hand on his shoulder, and looked across the table at Laurel. Laurel changed under her gaze. Her movements, as she ate her soup, grew slower, stolid. Time mapped its course beneath her eyes, along her mouth, spun a silver web over her chestnut hair. Corbet watched, motionless under the slender hand; I saw the longing for time kindle in his eyes.

Laurel, caught in his gaze, stared back at him out of aging eyes; he made a sound, twisting against the hand on his shoulder, but it did not yield to him.

"This," the woman said, her voice like high, sweet bells. She looked at me then. "And this."

Winds dragged at my hair, petals caught in it. Seams tore along my sleeves; my hands grew creased, dirty, my nails broken and black with earth. A strand of ashen hair blew into my bowl.

"Rois, your hair is in your soup," Laurel said patiently, as to a sick child or a wandering old woman. Her own hair was bone-white now, the skin puffed and sagging on her face. Only her eyes were familiar, still the same wide-set, smoky grey, though the faraway world they saw seemed imminent now, defined.

Still Corbet watched her, hungering for time. She smiled at him. Such a smile on any face is beautiful. His face changed again; a smile came out of him like light. I stared at my wrinkled hands; they closed like bird-claws around nothing.

I felt his eyes then, as if my clawed hands held his heart. "Rois," he said, and nothing more. I did not look at him; I did not know how to change the shape of his heart.

"Rois," Laurel said from the other side of that shadowland. "Are you all right?"

"She's eaten nothing," our father grumbled, and raised his voice. "Beda! Bring her some roast fowl." He poured more wine into my cup. The wine was blood-red now, and the cup fashioned of bone that had lain season after season in the wood, scoured clean by water and light. I drank it and heard Corbet say again,

"Rois."

I looked at him, finally. The woman had disappeared. Or perhaps she had changed into the rustling ivy sliding over his chair, until he was enthroned in green and bound to it, leaves circling his wrists and hair and throat. I stared, my heart aching at all that green shining in such a dreary season.

A shadowy Beda put something down in front of me; I started. Birds flew from my plate, leaving bone behind. Corbet made a soft sound. His eyes closed; he leaned back into the wood's embrace, all but vanishing into leaves.

"Rois," he whispered. And then, so faint I might only have heard him with my heart, "Please."

I felt the red rose bloom in my heart then; thorns

scored it, thorns pricked behind my eyes. I could no longer see him, only a blurred, fiery green. "All right," I said, to whatever he was asking, though I did not know why he wanted time and Laurel when he could have the timeless wood in all its mystery. "But I don't understand."

"I will show you," his heart's voice said, a promise or a warning. "If you will come with me."

"Rois," Laurel pleaded, "where are you? Are you wandering through the summer wood in winter? Corbet, call her back. She'll hear you. She must eat."

He said my name. I saw the candlelight glide along the silver in Laurel's hands; her hands were young again; so was her voice. I raised my head, saw our father's plump, anxious face, and Beda watching me, her fingers twisting the cloth of her apron. I looked at Corbet, for the green that had embraced him and bound him; green was a memory, a longing, nothing real in this dead world.

I picked up my fork, blinked at what lay on my plate. A chicken wing, my eyes told me finally, sprinkled with tarragon, a roast onion, braised carrots. I speared a piece of carrot grimly, as if I could pin the world into place on the end of my fork. "I'm all right," I said. "The wine made me dream."

"It'll take you like that," our father said, relieved, "on an empty stomach."

"Yes." It took as much effort to lift that carrot to my mouth as it would have to chop down a tree. It took more not to sit mutely staring at Corbet, waiting to be shown the tangled paths that lay behind his eyes.

I ate what I could, silently, keeping my eyes on my plate, while Corbet spoke to Laurel and our father, inviting, in his light way, tales of the past, of Laurel's childhood on the farm, memories of our mother, who was only a vague word or two, a touch, an indistinct face, in my own past.

"Laurel raised Rois," my father said, "though she was so young. She took to her responsibilities early. Beda did all she could, of course." He frowned at his plate; I wondered how much of her face he remembered by then, how much of his youth he had buried. "I was no help," he added, and sighed. "No help at all. I would look at Rois and see her mother's face, and that would be the last I could do. I let her run wild; I never checked her. She's been in and out of the wood in all seasons since she could walk."

As if he could have stopped me. I asked, to remind him I was still there, "Did she love the wood, too? Our mother?"

There was a little, odd silence, as if an answer hung between us in the candlelight, but no one would say it. Then Laurel and our father spoke at once.

"She took us walking in it—"

"No. She never went into it."

They stopped. I raised my eyes, found them looking perplexedly at one another. "But I remembered," Laurel said. "She would carry Rois—"

"While I was in the fields," our father interrupted a little abruptly. "It must have been. She seldom mentioned it." He studied his plate, jabbed without interest at a slice of onion. "Anyway, she never foraged, like Rois does. She never ran barefoot."

Laurel opened her mouth, closed it. Her eyes sought

Corbet's. Something passed between them, and the little, puckered frown appeared between her brows. She glanced at me, then at her plate; she changed the angle of her knife a degree or two, and finally spoke. "No," she said. "She wore shoes and only picked the wildflowers."

I wished I could remember. Corbet sat silently, his eyes on Laurel, then on our father, as if he could see what they did not say. I gave up trying to guess why our father took comfort in her shod feet.

"How did she die?" Corbet asked, with an unusual lack of grace, I thought. But our father seemed to want to talk about it. Perhaps he felt that Corbet should know these things about our family, our blameless, unmysterious past, but there his reasoning fell apart. He refused to consider that Corbet might be in love with Laurel, but that left me, his fey daughter who drank roses, an even more unlikely choice for the heir of Lynn Hall. He dreamed a double wedding in spring; he would be lucky, I thought starkly, to have one, and in this world.

"She died," he said heavily, "of some strange wasting illness. She could not eat. She fell sick during the autumn rains and died on the longest night of the year." He looked at me reproachfully; I stirred myself and ate another piece of carrot. "She had me shift her bed to the window so that she could look out. But there was nothing to see, just bleak winter fields and starless nights. I thought she watched for spring. But she died long before the crocus bloomed." He stared at his cup a moment. "Maybe it was not spring she watched for. Maybe she saw, finally, what she wanted; maybe she didn't. I'll never know."

"I'm sorry," Corbet breathed.

"At least I had my daughters to comfort me." He drank wine; the shadow eased out of his face. "My sweet Laurel and my wild rose." He smiled a little. "Rois kept bringing me things to cheer me up—some of them walked, I recall. A caterpillar, once, and a beetle with bright wings. A hummingbird's egg." He took a bite of chicken. "That was long ago."

"Your mother died young, too," I said abruptly to Corbet. "Do you remember her?"

He nodded. "Oh, yes. Very clearly." He touched his cup as if to lift it, but paused. His eyes, meeting mine, held a warning; I could almost hear the rustle of the ivy that held him in thrall. "She was tall, with very white skin. Her voice was gentle; she sang old ballads to me."

"How did—"

"I was never sure," he said, and drank before he continued, frowning a little, his eyes on the candle between him and Laurel. "For a long time, my father only said that she had gone away. He grieved terribly; he spoke very little, and I could not bear the look in his eyes when I asked about her. So I stopped asking. Years later, I asked; he only said that she had died, as his own mother had, of being too delicate to live in the world."

I swallowed dryly, pulling the husk loose from his answer to find the truth: She had been too human to live in the wood. Or too fey to live in the world.

Or was it all chaff? Had his true mother stood behind him with her skin as pale as moonlight, her hand on his shoulder, fingers flowing into the ivy that bound him to her world?

I watched him then, searching for her in his face, forgetting to eat while he watched Laurel, sometimes forgetting to eat, himself, at the way she spoke a word, or the way her face, under the shifting candlelight, changed every time she met his eyes. Our father, oblivious, and cheerful now, spoke of Perrin and his good nature, his hardworking ways, and of the grandchildren who were to overrun his old age.

"Eat," he urged me now and then. "Eat." But I could barely do more than watch the rich tapestry they wove of their glances and slow smiles, the words they spoke that said one thing to our father, and another to me, while the ivy, growing secretly all around us, whispered its warnings.

I bequeath all to the wood.

I drank more wine from my silver cup. It was pale sunlight now, and tasted of roses and blood. Snow whirled outside the window when we finished eating; Corbet, glancing out, said to Laurel,

"I should leave now. While I can."

"Yes," she said softly, and went to stand beside him, so closely they might as well have touched. "Later, it may not be possible."

"Perhaps it is no longer possible."

"Or course it is," our father said, lighting the iron lantern. "Only an inch or two on the ground yet. Follow the field wall when you leave the road—that will take you to the edge of the wood."

Corbet drew his eyes away from Laurel to look at me. "We Lynns walk on snow," he said, smiling; his eyes held no smile. I smiled back, learning from him and Laurel how to say secrets in idle commonplaces.

"What winter path will you take from place to place through the wood?"

"I'll dream one up," he said, and swung his dark cloak over his shoulders. He turned again to Laurel, his face set, withholding expression. "Thank you for asking me." He touched me lightly before he left. His fingers burned like the touch of the briers; I looked for the rose they must have left, but saw nothing. "Finish the wine," he suggested. "There are dreams and more in that."

And so I did. And so I dreamed his dream.

Fourteen

I stood in Lynn Hall.

Corbet was there and not there. A man with his face, a boy with his expressions, watched something bubble in a pot hanging over the fire in the marble hearth. The boy was small yet, slender, with dark hair and wide grey eyes; he stared at the pot, trembling a little in hunger, in anticipation. His coat of fine blue cloth was patched at the cuffs. He wore a thin quilt over his shoulders; it trailed on the marble floor behind him like a king's mantle.

The man turned away from the fire and began to pace. But not before I saw the fine honed bones of his face, the heavy-lidded eyes, the hair spun out of light. He drank from a silver cup; roses spiralled up its sides. He moved out of the circle of firelight into shadows disturbed only by a thin taper here and there. The winds shook the door until it rattled on its latch, wanting in; they reached down the chimney, but they could not get past the flames.

"Go and get more wood," Nial Lynn said. Tearle shrugged the quilt to the floor and turned without a word. Nial Lynn paced back into light, and I saw that his eyes were not green, but grey, like his son's, and his mouth was thin and bloodless, as if he never smiled, as if he drank the thorns out of his cup instead of roses.

The boy opened the door, struggling to keep it from crashing open against the stones. He went out in his frayed coat, without gloves, without a light. Nial Lynn paced. A taper guttered and went out. I could see no expression on his face; he seemed oblivious of himself, the pot over the fire, the storm, as if, in his own thoughts, he paced a different season, a different room.

The shadows fanned across the walls, deepening; I felt a chill where I stood, a shadow in a corner, or maybe only a taper's eye. The fire was consuming itself, and still Nial Lynn paced without a thought for the boy he had sent into the storm. It was not until fire crawled into the last glowing log and fumed that Nial seemed to see the dark around him.

He made an impatient noise, and kicked a flame out of the log with his boot. Then he went to the door and flung it open, calling. While he called, the boy, crouched against the door, slid into the room at his feet. Logs clattered out of his arms. He crawled, groping for them, shuddering. Nial Lynn reached for a log, tossed it into the fire, then, in the sudden brightness, resumed pacing, while the boy stumbled to his feet and brought the wood, piece by piece, to the fire.

Nial Lynn spoke finally. "Where were you?"

"I couldn't unlatch the door." He spoke without feeling, numb. "My fingers wouldn't move."

"We'll need more."

"I know." Tearle stood at the fire, his fingers under his arms, shivering. "I thought I saw things in the wind," he said after a moment. "Faces made out of wind and snow. Beautiful faces. Like my mother's."

"Perhaps you did," Nial Lynn murmured. "Perhaps you did." His eyes were very wide, his head uplifted, as if he searched the shadows for that face. He turned abruptly. Something happened; I couldn't see clearly. Nial Lynn stood near the door, his raised hand falling, and halfway across the room, at the hearth, Tearle lost his balance, fell against the pot above the fire.

It splashed him. I saw his mouth open, but he made no sound. He caught himself on the hearthstones before he fell into the fire. He leaned against them, trembling, holding one arm tightly, his eyes closed.

"She's gone," Nial Lynn said patiently. "Don't speak of her."

He did not speak again; the boy did not move for a long time, though I heard his harsh breathing. He moved finally, lifted a porcelain cup beside the hearth, to dip it into the pot. In the shadows, Nial Lynn turned again.

"No," he said, and the boy froze. "Bring more wood before you eat."

Tearle put the cup down without a sound, rose and went back into the storm.

When he had fought the door closed again, the

rooms grew black. I still heard the winds, whining and snarling. I shivered, chilled to the heart by the cold stones around me, the iron cold in Nial Lynn's voice. I saw Corbet, pacing the room as his grandfather had paced half a century before.

I knew him, though his back was turned, though the only light came from the blood-red rose burning on the hearth. I said his name, and in my dream he came to me. He did not touch me; we seemed to stand together in different times, his past, my dream. He knew me, though; he said, "Rois."

"What has this—" I could barely speak, shaking with the cold. "What has this to do with you? Why did you come back here?"

"To find my way out," he said simply. "You know that. Look."

He went to the door, opened it. I saw the boy crouched on the threshold again, weighed down by the wood in his arms, shivering too badly to stand. That is not what Corbet showed me. "Look," he said again, and I saw the riders in the storm.

They rode horses as white as hoarfrost. Snow and star and dark whirled around one another to etch a fine-boned face, eyes of night and crystal fire. Their mantles were of dark wind and snow; their wild hair caught snow and falling stars. The boy watched them, too, longing for their beauty, their mastery over cold and storm. *Come,* the winds called. *Come to us. This is not your true home. You belong elsewhere. You belong with us.*

"How?" I whispered; if I had not been dreaming, he never could have heard me. "How did your father find his way to them?"

He looked at me out of Nial Lynn's face, his cold secret eyes. "How did my grandfather?"

Snow misted off the roof between us; he blurred. I reached out to him, trying to catch a shadow. My hand closed on a knife-edge of wind. "How?" I asked again. I saw only the boy on the threshold, huddled against the door, clinging to wood, watching the faces of the storm.

I woke. It was still night; the winds in my dream sang their sweet, dangerous song around our house. *Come to us. Come.* Again I saw the frailness of our walls, how they could be broken by a thought, stone and board could sag like old web under a vision. I closed my eyes against the vision, and found my way back into the drift of leaves beside the well.

Laurel seemed to have heard those winds, too. Some dream had disturbed her calm; her face, paler than usual, wore an unfamiliar frown. When Perrin came in for breakfast, she looked at him for a moment as if she did not recognize him.

He had not slept well, either. "I kept hearing animals calling me from the barn—I'd wake and hear nothing but the wind." He brushed her cheek tentatively. "Are you all right?"

"Yes." She averted her face abruptly, left him blinking at her. She turned back quickly, feeling his dismay. "Those winds woke me as well. Only they had human voices."

"What did they say?" he asked, with an effort at humor. She only gazed through him.

"Nothing human," she said at last, and turned away again. "They left me out of sorts. I'm sorry. I didn't expect you this morning."

"I missed you," he said simply. He waited, holding the back of a chair as if for courage, while she stepped into the kitchen to tell Beda he had come. When she returned, he asked as simply, holding her eyes, "Was Corbet here last night?"

"Yes," she said, and the blood ran into her face, turning its winter pallor beautiful. His head bowed. He said nothing, just pulled out the chair in his hands to sit. I stepped into the room; his head lifted again.

"Rois," he said tonelessly, then made an effort. "You're looking better. Tired, but better." He stood up again suddenly. "Maybe I should help your father finish the milking—"

"Sit," Laurel said. She laid a hand on the crook of his arm. "Sit," she said gently. She did not meet his eyes, but her voice reached him. "These winter winds have us all confused. I barely know what I'm thinking or doing anymore."

"What shall I do?" he asked her softly. He slid his fingers beneath her wrist a moment. "What would you like me to do?"

"Just be patient with me. For now." Her voice made no promises.

"All right," he said steadily, and sat again, not so steadily. Beda came in with a great tray of eggs and sausage, bread, milk, butter, cheese and oatmeal porridge. She looked at our closed faces and heaved a sigh.

"These winds." She unloaded the tray, rattling crockery. "And this is only the beginning."

Corbet did not come for supper that night, only Perrin. That fretted both Laurel and me, though Laurel did her best to hide it. She sat beside the fire as usual, making lace, or at least making some attempt to move the hook occasionally. Perrin did not play. He tried to speak to Laurel; she answered absently, listening for another voice. At least I had him in my dreams, I thought; perhaps she did, too. But I hungered for his presence, his quick, riddling eyes that saw me more clearly than anyone had ever done, his lean, supple body, the questions he raised and left unanswered in the air, the glimpses he gave us of the world beyond our small lives, of a world even beyond that. Our father, fortunately, was in a talkative mood; he asked endless, detailed questions about Perrin's sick cows, until I could almost hear their plaintive bellowings and smell the barn. It made me want to walk into the snow, and keep walking, and keep walking, until I saw the faces in the wind and could follow them. Even Laurel looked haunted by her future; she threw Perrin a wide-eyed glance that he caught, mute and strained, while our father compared cow ailments.

Perrin left early; Laurel walked him to the door. It had stopped snowing; the moonlight tossed uneasy shadows on the silvery ground. Perrin brushed Laurel's lips with his; his eyes asked a wordless question. She seemed to have no answer; he turned away quickly. She watched him ride out of the yard. I lifted my face to the milky sky, but nothing rode that moonlit path to earth.

I asked Laurel later, when we turned down the lamps and banked the fire, "What will you do?"

The fierceness in her voice startled me. "I don't know," she said. "I do not know." She put a lamp down and opened a curtain, gazing at the moon above Corbet's wood. Her eyes glittered with tears of frustration, bewilderment; she gripped my wrist hard, as if she were falling, and looked at me finally. I did not recognize the expression on her face. "It's so hard to think in winter. The world seems confined in the space of your heart; you can't see beyond yourself. How can I change in a season what I have wanted for years? How can I bear to hurt Perrin?"

I was silent, chilled, remembering the rustling of the ivy in that room, those cold winter eyes. "You must wait," I forced myself to say, "until spring." *Until the curse is past,* I wanted to say. *Until we find the path out of the wood.* She listened to me, her eyes wide, intent, as if she thought I had pulled up wisdom along with the mandrake root. "You'll think more clearly then. And you'll know Corbet better."

She gazed at me, her fingers still tight on my wrist. "Rois," she whispered, and kissed me swiftly. I felt my throat burn. I shrugged impatiently, looking at candlelight, the moon, the white fields, anything but her face.

"It's you he wants. Not me. I know that. I have always known. But you must wait."

"How can I?" she demanded. "How can I sit night after night making lace for a wedding with a man I don't know if I can—"

"Hush," I breathed, hearing our father's step above our heads.

"And how can I tell him? Our father?"

"Don't. Don't tell him anything, not yet. You hardly know Corbet. He's a stranger; he'll catch at all our eyes until we're used to him, and by then maybe you'll—"

"No."

"You don't know him," I insisted. "He could hurt you."

She was silent again, her eyes wide, dark. "I know," she whispered, surprising me again. "He is such a mystery. He could pick my heart like a rose and watch it wither in his hand. Sometimes I think he is like that. At other times I think he is as simple and golden and generous as our father's fields. And then I see things in his eyes—things that I have never looked at, and I know that I have walked a short and easy road out of my past, while he has walked a thousand roads to meet me. I know Perrin's past; the same road runs into his future. I don't know Corbet. But I feel his hand upon my heart, and I wake wanting to say his name. I don't know, Rois, how much longer I can wait."

The hard winds sang their way into my dreams again that night. Long, white, insistent fingers of snow brushed against the window glass until I saw the storm out of memory, snow falling endlessly, hiding the moon, the earth, and any footprints in the frozen ground. *Come to us,* the winds called. *Come.* And I rose and saw the light from Lynn Hall flickering like a star among the wind-harrowed trees.

So I went there, walking through that wild storm,

scarcely feeling it, finding my way by the light I watched, the lodestar in the screaming night. Winds shook me apart piecemeal, flung a bone here, a bone there. My eyes became snow, my hair turned to ice; I heard it chime against my shoulders like wind-blown glass. If I spoke, words would fall from me like snow, pour out of me like black wind.

As I drew close to the light in the wood, I began to hear the words they spoke. Fear sharper than the cold shook through me, but I had to see, I had to know the path that Corbet Lynn had taken out of the world.

Winds shaped their voices—one desperate, wild, passionate, the other silken and biting, a blade of ice. Winds swirled into words; I did not want to hear them, but there was no place to hide, no haven but one from the storm they made between them.

You will never leave me, said the silken wind.

I am leaving you. Now. Watch me.

You will die out there.

You are colder than any winter night. You are more cruel than any wind.

I will not let you leave. The door will not open for you. The window will not break. There is no way out of here.

My mother found a way.

Wind roared through the dark; I caught a straining tree and clung to it. Birch, its smooth, papery bark told my cheek. I closed my eyes, felt the sting of snow against them, and heard a sound like ice shattering.

Then the winds died. Trees stood in a silence like the silence on the face of the moon. I turned, bewildered at first, then desperate; as I stumbled through the snow, the light seemed to move to meet me. And then the wind struck again, with terrible, icy force; I felt its bitterness in the hollows of my bones.

You will never find your way out of my heart.

The door opened; firelight fluttered across the threshold into the snow-streaked winds. I watched, trembling like the frail wings of light. A figure leaned against the doorway. I heard his uneven breathing, saw him racked with winds. He did not notice me as I crept out of the night into his shadow. His eyes clung to all the pale, beautiful riders in the wind.

Come, they said.

A horse as white as buttermilk came out of the dark, stood before him, looking at him out of still, onyx eyes. He mounted it. Then he bent down low, his hand outstretched to me.

"Rois," he said. I saw the color of his hair.

I drew myself up behind him, held him as tightly as any brier rose.

We rode into the winter wood.

Fifteen

I thought I knew what cold was, before cold stripped me bare of thought, then blinded me and froze my heart. I could not feel such cold and live; cold forced me into something other, something not quite human, who held a dream with bones of ice, and did not remember names, only what we once had been: a flower on a vine, a fall of light.

When I began to see again, as wind sees, or the moon, I had drawn cold as close to me as death. I did not feel it now, any more than ice feels the falling snow. Again I saw the elusive faces of wind and shadow, the wild riders of the night. An enchanted wood flowed past us. Trees, embraced by ice, spangled the night with whorls of crystal branches. The odd leaf that still hung on them flashed silver or gold like some strange jewel that only grew on trees, and only in the coldest night. Streams forged paths of wind-scoured silver through the snow, that grew harder, brighter, as we passed. Snow hares froze in our wake; the fox and weasel in their winter coats grew even whiter. We left no path for human eyes to follow beyond swirling, misty ribbons of snow. No one human watched us ride. Only the white owls saw us; only they followed.

Then we rode out of the heart of winter into light.

Light fashioned me into something more nearly human, and gave me back my memory. I had hair again, and skin; I had a name. But it could not reach my heart, still frozen by that cold, cold journey. I saw meadows and trees burning a young, fiery green, as if leaves had just opened, as if green itself had never existed before. I breathed heavy, golden air that might have pooled all summer over roses blooming in every color on a hundred trees. But I saw winter just beneath that scent, that green; I felt it just beneath my skin, and I didn't know anymore what I was, or if I was alive.

We had gone everywhere and nowhere; we had ridden from Lynn Hall to Lynn Hall. But in this unfamiliar country, the house was as I had only seen it in a dream. The buttermilk mare, following a single hooded rider on a horse as black as nothing, brought us back to the door we had left. Other riders flowed away from us, making little more noise than leaves; they went elsewhere, into the wood, maybe, or back into the wind. The hooded rider dismounted at the door; so did Corbet, slipping suddenly out of my hands. I felt something tear at my heart then, as if it had broken from the cold.

"Corbet," I whispered, as he turned toward the stranger. "Where are we?"

He looked up at me, his eyes empty of all expression; he seemed as far from me as he could go without leaving me. "This is the place where I was born."

The hooded rider loosed his cloak, shrugged it away from him like some winter skin, and I saw his face.

Stunned, I felt his name in my throat, though I had only seen him in a dream, or in other people's memories. His face had shed its childhood by a dozen years, grown leaner, harder. But I recognized that long dark hair, those eyes as grey as fieldstone that changed like water changes with every shift of cloud. He must have worn that face when he fled out of time after he killed Nial Lynn; it had been honed to an inhuman beauty and trapped there. I heard Corbet draw breath slowly, as if to still a fear, or gather calm against a storm.

"Welcome home," his father said, and went up the steps into the house. Corbet turned away from me, left me his shadow to follow.

Doors were flung wide in this house; nothing was barred, nothing nailed shut. Rooms wandered into other rooms; light spilled through silk and linen, gilding marble floors. The summer breeze scattered the scents of roses, grasses, wildflowers everywhere. I heard voices in the garden, laughing, speaking lightly; I could not hear the words; perhaps I couldn't understand them. Inside the house, I heard steps, a call, a door opening, closing. I saw no one.

Corbet stood in front of a familiar hearth. I went to

him, wanting fire, or at least a little human warmth. But the grate was cold and gleaming, and the barest recognition was all I got from him. Roses the color of new blood lay carelessly on the mantel behind him. Above us hung a tapestry of silver and gold and palest green that in my world had faded into white: a great oak so entwined with ivy it had died, its bare branches pushing through the leaves like bone. I stared at the roses, wanting to hold my hands to such red, but like the light, they burned cold.

Air above the empty, polished grate ignited suddenly; I stepped back, startled, and turned to see Tearle Lynn close his hand and let it fall.

"She is trembling," he said to Corbet.

"In her world, it is still winter."

"She should have left cold behind her."

"It isn't easy," Corbet said. "I tried."

His father made a soft noise, part laughter, part contempt; his eyes grew nearly black with bitterness. "You could have gone anywhere. Why did you waste time in the past?"

"I couldn't find my way out of it." He spoke steadily, evenly, but his face was colorless as bone. He watched his father carefully, as if Tearle might vanish and reappear out of Corbet's shadow; as if he might lift a careless hand across the room and crack the stone at Corbet's back. "You never did."

Tearle shifted restively, a young man's protest against a meaningless argument. "The human world is a cold and bitter place; nothing lasts in it. You must know that by now. You were nearly trapped there in its deadliest season. What did you imagine you were doing in those two rooms? Trying to turn yourself human?"

"Yes," Corbet said, so simply that for a breath he rendered his father incapable of moving. Then Tearle brushed away the noise his son had made, and paced a step or two.

"You have learned better, I hope. In that place things begin to wear away even as they are built; the living die a little more each day. The sun is too far away; light slides endlessly into night; fire and love consume themselves; the heart tries to warm itself with ashes. I brought you up in a world of changeless beauty. I could understand more easily if you had lingered for human love in a place that made some feeble attempt to reflect this. But instead you found the rotting bones of Nial's house and crawled into his heart. Why? You knew we would come for you when you stayed too long. Why did you force me to find you there? What did you think you would find among my memories?"

Corbet's hands clenched suddenly on nothing. He whispered, "Hope."

"There?" his father demanded incredulously. His voice had risen only slightly, but something—anger or fear—snapped through the air around him. "The only hope I found in that house was death."

"How like mortals," Corbet breathed, "to confuse the two." Then his rigid face broke open, freeing expressions I had never seen; words, shaken loose by his father's storm, came out of him in a sudden, desperate cry. "I hoped for something true! Something from my hands, from my heart, not Nial's, not yours. I wanted to rebuild this house in the human world, with time, with earth, with new wood—"

"Why? When you have this house already, and in this world?"

"It's not mine, it's not yours; it's Nial Lynn's cold, cruel, loveless house—you brought everything he gave you with you when you ran."

"I brought nothing with me from that world!"

"Yes! You brought nothing! That was all he gave you!" Tearle opened his mouth to answer; nothing came out. He looked astonished, as if Corbet himself had spun the soft summer air into lightning. "This is still Nial's house. You don't feel the cold here because that's all you ever knew. You learned no human warmth from him, you only glimpsed it in others' faces, beside other fires that warmed more than the air they touched. In the end you ran to what you knew best, instead of into the human world, where no one would have blamed you—"

"No one helped me when he was alive," Tearle said. "And when he died, I no longer needed help." His eyes were very wide, a silvery sheen flashing across the grey, like ice or tears. There were warnings in his tense muscles, in his brittle words. "I left that world, and all I could of memory, behind me. Here I dreamed the house that Nial hated, opened the doors and rooms he nailed shut, and found a human who had fled her world to live with me—"

"Did she truly escape what she ran from when she ran here to you? Or is that why she died so young here, because, like you, she found her only hope in death?"

His father did not answer in words; he barely moved. Corbet flung back his head abruptly, a sound breaking out of him; the imprint of a hand left a thorn of blood beside his mouth.

"Your mother came to me freely," Tearle said fiercely. "She stayed here freely— "

"No one does." Corbet's voice shook. "Look at the price you paid to come here. You took your father's life, now you have his house and all his power. My mother died of winter in this summer world, and so will any mortal maid die who follows me here expecting human love. That's why I tried to stay in the human world, why I tried to love there. But— "

"Is that all I gave you?" Tearle took a step toward Corbet, looking unexpectedly lost, as if he had finally stumbled onto the twisted path his son travelled. "Is that all I gave your mother?"

Corbet drew breath to answer. Then he closed his eyes and drew breath again. "Why do you think I left this place?" he whispered. "Why do you think I left? You gave us all you could. You gave me a glimpse of all you really wanted, and where I might go to find it. I tried to find that place, I tried to build a house, love a woman in the world where things are always dying, and there is never enough time. But all I did was rebuild Nial Lynn's house, and open his door, and find you waiting to take me back."

Without moving, Tearle stepped into human time; I saw the young boy's eyes, filled with terrible, hopeless longing for what he saw but never had. Then he opened a hand, slapped the memory away with the power that had replaced hope. Corbet stood motionless, holding his father's gaze, while all around us and above us doors and windows closed, echoing one another through the house like a long roll of thunder. Wind roiled through the ivy in the tapestry; I heard leaves chatter.

"I know that world too well," Tearle said succinctly. "And you have learned too much."

"You knew—" Corbet stopped, started again, hopelessly. "You knew a piece of it."

"All anyone ever knows, in that timebound place. You will stay here." His eyes flicked to me. "She will stay with you. Whatever she is. She has followed you this far out of her world. But she hasn't followed you blindly. She has our eyes. Perhaps," he added grimly, "being more than mortal, she will not confuse death with hope."

I felt the ice again, beneath my skin, at the core of my thoughts. I tried to shape words; they eluded me. There were too many, or too few, to answer what I thought I had heard. Corbet, gripping stone, seemed to have the same trouble untangling words.

"No," he said breathlessly. "She cannot stay."

"Why not? She's here. She has eyes that see beyond the human world; she must have inherited them from someone. As I did. And you. She didn't stray here out of innocence. She was looking for this place."

"I wasn't—" I began, but I heard the lie before I finished. I had searched for it, behind the tapestry, within the reflection in the razor's edge. I had known . . . My hands lifted, reaching for Corbet, for mortal flesh and bone. But his hand slid from the mantel; he moved away from the hearth and my fingers closed on air before I touched him. He went to Tearle, each step on the gleaming marble sounding longer than the last, until it seemed he had crossed some vast wasteland to reach his father. "This place is very beautiful," he said softly. "And you did give me something of great value. You gave me a dream to take with me into the human world. You gave me far more than your father ever gave you. But I can't stay here. You fought for your freedom and won a different kind of prison. I will fight for mine—"

"You can't fight me," Tearle reminded him harshly.

"I know." In the placid light, his face looked chilled and very weary. "But I can die."

There was silence within the hall and without. No voices called lightly across distances; no birds sang. Everything listened, it seemed, even stone and air. Tearle held words locked in his hands, in his tight mouth, in his eyes, as he stared at his son. Corbet did not move or speak; he simply waited for his father to find a word to free them both.

She came out of nowhere, shaping herself out of air and light and the barren midnight I saw in her eyes. Winter followed her; I felt the icy glide of air along my skin; I smelled it. Her long dark hair, tossed by the winds of a deadly season, tangled wildly around her. Winds tugged at her skirt and trailing sleeves, revealing winter faces: a dark eye, a clawed and bloody paw, a white wing. She looked at me and smiled. Her teeth were pointed like an animal's, and her sapphire eyes flared like stars. I wanted to melt into the stones behind me, crawl among the shadows in the chimney. Even the fire had frozen in her smile. She turned away from me and showed a different face to

Corbet, a different season, one I had no name for; the brief, sweet seasons in my small world could only hint at it.

"Clouds have formed above the meadow," she said. "And all the birds in the garden are gone." She touched Corbet lightly; her long fingers closed around his wrist. "You lingered in the human world too long; you are behaving like a human."

He did not look at her; he held his father's eyes. He said to both of them, "I will not stay."

"And I will not let you leave me." Her tranquil voice carried a warning to them both. She answered Corbet, but turned her dark, unblinking gaze on Tearle until she had his attention and his eyes. "Tell him so. Tell him that he will never leave us."

"I will not stay."

"Tell him that I can keep him past death: His ghost will wander forever through my seasons. Death leads nowhere but to me. Tell him."

Expression emptied out of Tearle's eyes, left an opaque mist. Corbet trembled suddenly, as if he too felt the gnawing winds. Then I could no longer see his face; it blurred under my tears. Her attention seized me, swift and predatory, sensing any mortal warmth.

"Who is this, weeping at my hearth? I remember you. You saw me once or twice before. I thought you were some farmer's lovesick child. Look at me. Let me see your eyes."

I would rather have stared down a raging blizzard until it blinded me. But I seemed helpless under the force of her regard; her eyes seemed everywhere, even behind my closed eyes. I opened them finally, and fell into some vast, blank shadow, the dark side of the moon.

"Rois."

The shock of my name in this strange world brought me back to it: a lovesick farmer's daughter who had wandered out of the world to hear her name spoken by the queen of summer and winter and the harvest of the dead. Her eyes had narrowed at what she saw. I felt the rattling icicle fingers of the wind again, and I wondered if, like the winter here, I had turned white to match her cold.

She said softly, "You see too much. Who gave you your eyes?" I couldn't speak; I could only stay frozen and mute under her hawk's stare, hoping that if I did not move she would think me something not worth the effort. She loosed me abruptly and turned, but I was no longer safe. "I will keep you here. You belong with me."

"No," Corbet said quickly. "Rois doesn't belong here; she is mortal—"

"Then why did you bring her? If you don't want her?" He found himself wordless; she smiled a fine, sweet smile. "You brought her because you think she sees what you cannot. You are wrong. There is no way out of my heart for either of you."

He moved, pulling so fiercely against her hold that he startled her: the seasons in her changed again, revealing the wildness beneath the summer light. Her fingers turned to thick tree roots; she shook him to his knees. She spread her other hand across his face and left a mask of ice; his mouth opened, froze into a silent scream.

Tearle moved. That's all I saw, before winter raged through the house. Winds shrieked like ravens; the frozen fire broke into pieces on the grate. Ghosts spun out of blown snow snatched at my eyes, my breath. I thought I heard voices, but they kept weaving into wind. The winds grew owls' feathers, owls' claws, and streaked across my eyes. I felt my bones change into air, into stone, into ice, until I heard my own voice crying one word that turned me human again,

"Corbet!"

I heard a single winter *Rois* among the deadly voices of the winds.

I stumbled to my feet, fought toward him through her winter, reaching out to him at every step, though her winds sealed my eyes shut and I had only my heart to see with. I could not find him, though I ran beyond winter into silence; my hands held only longing. Finally even my heart's eye closed in the bitter dark; I fell into the embrace of stone.

Sixteen

I woke to the sound of Salish's voice.

What Salish was doing in my bedroom I could not imagine. Then I felt the hard, cold bed I lay on, and I lifted my head, stared at white marble. I dropped my head again, groaning, making sense of nothing.

"Rois," Salish pleaded. He dropped something over me; I smelled damp wool, fur. "Rois. Please wake up."

I did, so suddenly I startled him. Memory came back, not piecemeal like a dream, but whole and stark. I had been in Lynn Hall; I was still in Lynn Hall. I had lost Corbet in the wrong hall. I tried to get up; my bones had turned to marble against the stone, too awkward and heavy to lift.

"Are you hurt?" Salish asked. His voice wavered oddly. He was wavering, too; I blinked him into focus.

His face, a younger, more stolid version of Crispin's, was patchy with fear; he looked close to tears.

"No. Just frozen."

"Well, what are you doing here in Lynn Hall freezing next to a dead body?"

I felt my heart flare painfully, breaking or coming back to life. I pushed myself up, and blood pricked through me again. I could not find my voice.

Corbet's father lay beside me on the hearthstones. He looked like something frozen in time, encased in a sheen of frost. Even the blood that had flowed from his head glittered icily on the white marble. His eyes were open; they held a faint glaze of horror, as if he had glimpsed these two rooms as he died. His elegant clothes belonged in a different season; his fine, eerie beauty belonged anywhere but in our small world.

She had killed him; she had flung him here like a dead animal, a message, a warning. I put my hands to my mouth, beginning to shake, feeling her eyes everywhere. I had found my way out of her world when she had said there was no way out. *I know your world*, her message said. *I know your tales. I am in your winter.*

"Rois." Salish touched my shoulder. "Who is he?"

I moved my hands, folded them tightly, trying to think. "I just came to see Corbet. I built a fire. I must have fallen asleep beside it, waiting."

"He never came?"

"No."

"Well, where is he? And who is this dead on his hearth, dressed for spring? How did you get here? I didn't see your horse."

"I walked."

His voice rose. "Through that storm?"

Pinwheels of fire sparked behind my eyes. "Don't shout—"

"He's not likely to wake up, is he? He must have walked as well; he didn't leave a horse in the stable. The door's wide open; there's nothing in there but snow. You didn't see this one come in?"

I shook my head, burrowing deeper into Salish's cloak. Beneath the fur, I could reach out, touch a motionless shoulder. He had fought her for Corbet's sake and died. He must not have yielded easily; she had left him where she had found him, in the place he hated most.

"You didn't hear the fight?"

I stared at Salish. Then I saw, beyond him, the shards of crystal scattered on the floor, candles knocked out of their sconces, a lamp on its side in a pool of oil.

"Someone left the door open," I said uncertainly. "The winds got in."

"This one left it open when he came in? Dressed like he is? Or Corbet left it open when he came and went?"

"I don't know." I rubbed my eyes, feeling tangled in my own lies; I had said what I thought was easiest to believe, but even I wasn't finding it easy. "What are you doing here?" I asked wearily. If Salish had not come, I could have just gone home, leaving the mystery behind me for someone else to find.

"I brought some things Corbet wanted from the inn. I didn't see any smoke from the chimney, but I thought I'd leave them anyway . . . Looks like he hit his head, falling." He paused briefly. "Or he was hit and fell. Rois—"

He paused again, swallowing, not looking at me, his eyes on the dead man's face. "You didn't—he didn't—" His eyes came back to me, pleading. "Did you?"

It might have made things easy again: I had found the young stranger there instead of Corbet, he had attacked me when I refused him, we had brawled among the crystal, I had pushed him and he fell. But, looking at the still face, all I saw was Corbet's father, who had fought for his son and lost. I could never tell such lies about him.

I shook my head, swallowing sudden tears. "I never saw him before in this world." I struggled to my feet. Then I had to fold myself again, bone by bone, to close his eyes, so he would no longer have to see the cruel place he had fled.

By the time we crossed my father's fields in Salish's sleigh, I could barely see past the pounding in my head. The fields seemed yet another boundary between worlds; I remembered Laurel then, and our father, and I wondered what they must be thinking. Maybe they hadn't noticed me missing. The sun had barely risen; my father would still be in the barn. Laurel might have called me and thought me elsewhere, but only in the bath, or in the barn, or even out wandering in the quiet morning. But I saw the tracks of our sleigh in the fresh snow as Salish turned into the yard, and Laurel had flung open the door and come out before he pulled to a stop.

"Rois!" She was shivering, her cheeks flushed with anger and relief and cold. "Where have you been all night?" Her eyes went to Salish then, and widened. Salish ducked nervously into his hood.

"I'll leave you here," he told me gruffly, "and find someone in the village to go and deal with the other."

"The apothecary," I suggested, and he nodded. I untangled myself stiffly from his furs and rugs, and climbed out into Laurel's confusion, which I could feel, like heat from glowing embers, from the bottom of the steps.

"Our father took the sleigh to get Perrin," she said, "to help him look for you." Her eyes were red with sleeplessness, the skin drawn taut across her face. She added, controlling exasperation, "We thought of course of Lynn Hall. But there was no smoke this morning, so we thought Corbet must have gone to the inn to wait out the storm. We thought that's where you might be." Her voice trailed; her eyes strayed again to Salish, who could not seem to find his reins among his furs. Unwilling to upset Laurel farther with a dead body, he was waiting for me to mention it. But I didn't know how to tell her, either, or even what.

I said tiredly, "Thank you, Salish."

He lifted the reins reluctantly. "If I see your father, I'll tell him you're home."

I followed Laurel into the house. I was shivering badly, even in the warmth; things kept blurring in the fire behind my eyes. I fumbled with my cloak ties, managed to pull them into a knot. I felt Laurel's fingers move between mine, work at it. "Were you with Salish?" she asked, without much hope; nothing could be that simple.

"I was at Lynn Hall."

Her fingers stilled. "Oh, Rois," she breathed. I put my hands over my eyes, struggling between words, between tales.

"I had a dream of Corbet—I couldn't sleep after it. I had to see—"

Her voice came back abruptly, rising, and I winced. "How did you get there?"

"I walked."

"Through that storm? How?"

"I don't know how—maybe I was still dreaming—"

"No wonder you look half dead. So of course he wouldn't have sent you home until morning—but why didn't he bring you himself?"

I dropped my hands, remembering where I had left Corbet. "He wasn't there."

"He wasn't—" Laurel stared at me. "You stayed all night in that empty place?"

I nodded, not trusting my voice, looking everywhere but at her so that she would not see in my eyes what I had seen. She loosed the ties finally, pulled my cloak off.

"He must be at the inn," she said slowly, troubled without knowing why, by all the things I had not told her. "Rois, are you all right?"

"My head aches."

"Go to bed. I'll bring you some tea."

I smelled roses as I walked into my room. I stopped, beginning to shiver again, from more than cold, as I stared at them. They lay scattered all over the floor, the blood-red roses I had seen on the mantel in Lynn Hall. They had dried, passing between worlds, neither alive nor dead: another message. *I know where you are,* they said. *I know what you love. I know you.*

I undressed and crawled under the quilts, pulled

them over my head, trying to quiet pain and think. I slipped so easily into her world then, with Corbet beside me and Tearle still alive, that I wanted to weep when Laurel's step woke me. I could not find my way back in dreams, I knew then. They were memory and desire, terror and hope; they told me only what I already knew.

Laurel set the tea down and felt my face. "You're burning."

"I got too cold in that house . . ."

"I can't believe you even found it in that storm, without freezing to death first. You must have dreamed your way there."

"Maybe."

She picked up my clothes and folded them slowly, her mind elsewhere, not on me or my untidy room, but on Corbet, I guessed, by the faint worry in her eyes. He had not been where I had dreamed him . . . She didn't question the dried roses all over the floor; she simply gathered them up, too, as if they were laundry. She asked finally, "Rois, what did you dream that made you run through a storm to Lynn Hall?"

I struggled up, reached for the tea, held the warm cup a moment against my head. "It was more a feeling," I said finally, "that something was wrong."

She gazed at me over the roses. "With Corbet? Was he hurt? Lost in the snow?"

I took a sip of tea, swallowed a scalding *yes*. "He was—I was dreaming of Nial Lynn's curse. I thought Corbet was in trouble. That's why I went there."

"That curse." She looked vaguely at the roses in her hands. "You've been haunted by it." The little line had formed between her brows. She didn't know which of us to worry about now: the woman obsessed by imaginary curses, or the man cursed by them. She dropped the roses into an empty pitcher and glanced out the window at the blank sky above the wood. Still undecided, she straightened the quilts around me. "Try to sleep. I'll find out where Corbet is."

I slept until a white owl with sapphire eyes glided noiselessly out of the white sky to stare at me through the window. I woke with my heart pounding, heaving quilts aside as I rolled to face the window. I saw nothing except what might have been, to my sleep-blurred eyes, a reflection of white disappearing against the clouds. I heard strange noises, though, which separated into voices as I listened, and then into words.

I got out of bed, went to the window. The cold glass against my face cleared my head a little; so did the scene below.

Laurel was sitting in our sleigh, holding the reins and trying to move, while Perrin, holding the plow horses' heads, argued with her down their backs. His own horse, hock-deep in snow, nuzzled at his back. Their voices, normally so patient, sounded ragged, barely restrained. Our father, astounded and forgotten, stood watching near the house below me.

"This is nothing," Perrin said doggedly. "It's seasonal. It will pass. You've loved me and I've loved you since—"

"People change," Laurel said without sympathy.

"Not in a season! Not over the color of a head of hair!"

"It isn't that—Perrin, it's more, much more—you've seen! All winter long, you've watched us—"

"For years I've watched us—you and me. Is that worth nothing to you? You can't just pull love to a halt like a horse and a harrow—all I'm asking is that you wait. Just give yourself time. Give me time."

"For what?" she demanded helplessly, flicking the reins a little; the horses, trying to go and stay at once, pushed, startled, against Perrin. He caught his balance, held them stubbornly. "How much longer do you want to sit there in the evenings, watching Corbet and me watching each other? Watching me smile at him instead of you? Watching—" She gestured again, carelessly.

Perrin finished grimly: "Watching you with him thc way you used to be with me."

She bowed her head; I could not see her face. Suddenly frightened for her, I tried to open the window. She would only find winter, I wanted to tell her; she would have to go beyond the world she knew to find Corbet. Winter had sealed the window shut. Perrin stood mute, clinging to the horses, while she let the reins fall slack in her hands. She spoke finally; I couldn't hear. But I could guess: *I can't help myself.*

"I'm sorry," she said more clearly. He did not answer, did not move. "Perrin. If he's not in the village and not in his house, maybe he left some message in Lynn Hall, some hint of where he is."

"Rois was just there, you said—"

"How much could she see in the dark?"

"Let me go instead."

"I'm going," she said flatly. I pounded desperately on the thick glass, but she was not listening to anything but herself. "And you must let me go. Can't you understand that waiting will not change the way I love? Maybe you and I are too much alike. Maybe if it hadn't been Corbet Lynn, it would have been someone else—"

Perrin moved abruptly; so did the horses. "Don't say that," he said sharply. "Don't toss me away so cheaply. Neither of us has a wayward heart. We love what we love and that's that. That's why you should wait, test whatever this is you think is love—"

She brought the reins down hard then, and he lurched backward. He loosed the horses; she turned them, edged them around him until they faced the road and she had brought the sleigh up to where he stood.

"Love is what we say it is," she said fiercely. "That's all I know. That's all anyone knows about it. I'm sorry."

He must have seen something in her face, some breath of indecision, in spite of everything. He said recklessly, "Then let's hear what Corbet Lynn knows about it," and pulled himself into the sleigh beside her, even as she brought the reins down again, and the runners sheared a path out of the yard toward Lynn Hall.

I went back to bed. I heard my father's heavy tread on the stairs, slower and quieter than usual, even through my dreams. It stopped at my door. I woke again, near dusk, and heard him talking to Beda. I sat up and finished my cold tea, still listening, but I heard no other voices. The relentless pain in my head had finally subsided. My thoughts cleared enough to show me what I had to do in the next moment at least, which was to go downstairs and talk to my father before Salish's tale, transformed into who knew what wonders on its way through the village, got to him before I did.

I found him beside the fire, brooding over his cold pipe. He looked startled at my wild hair, my red eyes, but he lifted one arm bravely and I sat next to him, dropped my head against his shoulder.

"I'm sorry," I said wearily.

"Sorry! Sorry can't speak to this. You could have died out there."

"I know."

"Laurel said you were dreaming—walking in your sleep. How could anyone sleep through that kind of weather?"

"Is she back yet?"

He shook his head, chewed hard on his pipe a moment. "She went off to look for Corbet," he said finally, "with Perrin along for the ride. Corbet Lynn." He didn't like it, but he could not say why. "Did you see that coming?"

"From the first."

"I never saw it coming . . . Maybe Perrin is right," he added without hope. "Maybe it will blow itself out by spring."

"Maybe. If she finds Corbet."

"Oh, he's around somewhere." He cheered up a little. "Maybe with some other woman. How far could anyone have got to in that storm?"

"Maybe," I said again. I shifted, wondering how to begin. "Did you see Salish this morning?"

"Salish? No. Laurel said he found you."

"He found me, yes. He also—he also found a stranger in Lynn Hall. On the hearth. He was—he died there."

My father's arm slackened on my shoulders. He pulled back a little, staring at me. "What?"

"Corbet Lynn was gone. Someone died in his house last night. Salish left me here and went into the village to get the apothecary—"

"What?" His voice rose. "What are you talking about? Laurel didn't say—"

"Laurel didn't know. I didn't tell her. My head hurt, I couldn't think, and there was nothing she could have done—"

"Who died? How did he die?"

"I don't—it looked like an accident. He might have fallen and hit his head on the stones. He was—"

"Did you see it happen?"

"No. I woke and he was there beside me on the floor."

"What are you telling me?" my father demanded sharply. "That someone died beside you while you were sleeping and you never noticed? Where was Corbet during all this? Some stranger walked into his house while he was away and dropped dead on his hearth? In the middle of a blizzard?"

"So it—" I paused, trying to swallow my own tale. "That's what it seemed—"

The door opened abruptly; Laurel came in, with Perrin close behind her. She didn't bother taking off her snow-crusted cloak; she came to us quickly, dripping and shivering, her eyes luminous and strained from trying to see beyond the world.

"Rois." She gripped my hands. "What exactly did you dream?"

The blood pounded into my head; her face blurred. I told her what she already knew. "That he left Lynn Hall."

"You didn't find Corbet," our father said flatly. Perrin shook his head.

"The place is cold, the stable is empty." He stopped, started again. "It seems there was an accident—"

"I know—Rois has been—he's not in the village?"

Laurel put a hand to her mouth. "No." Her voice shook badly; kneeling close to the fire, she still shivered. "He's nowhere. He didn't even leave a message—"

"He just left a dead man on his hearth? Did anyone recognize him? He must have had a horse, belongings with him. Nobody wanders around on foot in a blizzard. Except Rois."

"He didn't—there was nothing . . ." Perrin's voice trailed away again; he shook his head, his mouth tight. My father asked again,

"Did anyone recognize him?"

"Well—that's just it. He must be some relation to Corbet, though they don't look at all alike." I stared at Perrin, amazed. "A brother, maybe, or a cousin, which makes things messier. But—"

"But what?" my father pleaded.

For once in his life, Perrin seemed reluctant to share gossip, even in the dead of winter, when there was nothing else to do. "Well, you know how news runs through the village, especially when everyone's out shovelling after a storm. But the oldest swear that's who surfaced out of their past to die where his father died—it's who he must look like, anyway—"

My father's face smoothed in utter astonishment. "You can't mean—"

"Nial Lynn's son."

In the silence, Laurel got to her feet unsteadily. Perrin reached out to her, but she did not notice. She went to the window, stood staring out. I saw the tears in her eyes finally melt, catch light as they slid down her face. She made no move to brush at them; she made no sound. She stood there, watching for Corbet, while Perrin watched her, and I heard the deadly winds ride toward us across the fields.

Seventeen

All night I heard them call me. In my dreams they cried my name in Corbet's voice; awake, in the dark, I listened to her voice, the whisper of snow against glass, the murmuring and sudden, furious whine in the eaves. Sometimes I heard Laurel's quiet, disconsolate weeping weaving into the winds, until it sounded as if she were out among them, a ghost of herself, mourning another ghost. I realized, in those black hours, that I didn't know if Corbet was alive or dead. He had threatened; she had said . . . But it was Tearle's body that she had left for us to find in the dead of winter, wearing his cursed, ambiguous face, trouble for Corbet to explain in our world if he managed to escape the trouble in hers.

I had to find him. I had gone into her world and come out of it once; I could do it again, though I didn't know how, or where, or what she would do when she saw me, except smile with her sharp white teeth and break my heart like a bone between them.

In the morning, I found Laurel at the same window, watching the motionless fields. If I hadn't heard her sobbing in her bed, I would have thought she had been there all night. Her pale, still face, her wide eyes that had always seemed to gaze beyond the world, frightened me; this emptiness was what they had found at last. She looked spellbound by Corbet's absence, even more surely than she had been by his presence. But our father, coming in from milking, only shook his head and refrained from calling her to breakfast.

"It's the shock," he said to me. He looked hollow-eyed himself, with daughters and neighbors disappearing in the night, a stranger with a face out of the past dying in a cursed house, lovers quarrelling, and whatever apple brandy he had drunk to comfort himself burning behind his eyes. He added, "At least when she tried to send Perrin away, he had more sense than to go."

I took my eyes away from the pale, still face of winter watching Laurel, and stared at my oatcakes, trying to think of some excuse to leave the house.

"I should go to the apothecary's," I said finally, "while the weather is holding."

He lifted his head sharply. "What for?"

"Something I need for Laurel. It will help her sleep. She can't go on like this."

"She'll get over it, and you've got every tea and root and dried weed—"

"He sends for things I can't find."

"No."

"He may have news of Corbet. They may have found out who the stranger is."

He hesitated, as curious as anyone; his "No" came with less conviction. He must have seen that I would go, anyway; I would walk if I could not ride, I would go barefoot if he hid my boots. How far I would go, he did not want to ask. He pointed his fork at me.

"I want you there and back in the same morning and in the same set of tracks."

I lied; he was suspicious. But it was better, he must have thought, than having two daughters waiting mute and red-eyed at the window for a man who might be anywhere. He watched me turn the sleigh down the road toward the village instead of across the field to Lynn Hall. I watched half-a-dozen sleighs laying tracks toward the hall, overladen with searchers, snowshoes, and more than likely the beer they hadn't finished through the night. They were looking for the path the wind had taken, I could have told them—the place where roses bloomed in snow. But they would never listen to me; they would go on searching snowdrifts for a man frozen to death in a storm, or his horse, or the stranger's horse and his possessions, or any scrap of his cloak to tell them that he had not really wandered out of summer into Lynn Hall.

Blane, the apothecary, looked surprised to see me. "What are you doing out of bed?" he asked. "Salish said he found you nearly frozen on a slab of marble; he thought you had died, too."

"I came back," I said tiredly. He eyed me closely, but did not ask from where. "I need something for Laurel."

"Laurel?"

"Is there any news of Corbet?" Maybe, I thought without hope, she had cast him adrift in time and winter, to account on human terms for the dead man in his house. Blane shook his head.

"Nothing. But they've barely begun to search. What's wrong with Laurel?"

"She's having trouble sleeping."

He grunted and finished straining a tincture into a bottle. "She's not the only one. I've had all the old folk in the village who can still walk in here this morning, wanting to tell me their nightmares, wanting potions and gossip, wanting to see the face of the man they think they recognize after fifty years."

My eyes slid past him to the closed door of the room where he examined the dead and prepared them for burial. I felt my eyes burn, and swallowed words because I could not say them, and sorrow because she left him for us to bury in the smallest room, in a world he hated. Maybe she had kept his ghost.

"Rois. Do you want to see him again? Is there something you need to tell?"

I looked at Blane. His lean face was ageless in a birdlike way, without a line to spare on it. His eyes, pale and cool, had seen our lives by daylight and by the dark of the moon; there was nothing that he hadn't heard by now. Almost nothing. And I knew exactly what would go into the potion he would make me if I told him.

"No," I sighed. "I wish I could be more help. I heard they think it's Corbet's brother."

"That's not what they think, the oldest of them." He

corked his bottle and picked up wax to seal it. "They think it's Corbet's father. And that Corbet killed him and fulfilled the curse and vanished."

"But—"

"I know, it makes no sense, but the oldest memories are the clearest, at that age, and they all remember Nial Lynn's tormented son. There's no getting around one dead man in Lynn Hall and another vanished: an echo out of the past."

I asked hollowly, "Did you find signs that he was murdered?"

He shrugged slightly, baffled. "He may have been struck before he fell. Maybe his heart stopped and he hit his head falling. There are no other signs of violence. Maybe he simply did not get out of the cold fast enough . . . He came out of the storm, saw your embers, left the door open behind him and fainted on the hearth. The wind got in, threw a few things around, and Salish found you both. It could be that simple. Except—"

"Except."

"Where on earth is Corbet? And if he did kill the stranger, why didn't he just bury the body in the woodpile until spring? We'd all be sleeping better."

"What are you going to do with the body? The only place you can bury him, with all this snow, is in the family vault with Nial Lynn."

The apothecary snorted. "I'm not going to put anyone wearing that face in with Nial Lynn. I wouldn't trust either of them to stay dead. I'll put him in the icehouse out back. Someone will most likely come looking for him soon and solve our mystery for us." He turned, set the tincture on the shelf behind him. "Now, what can I give you for Laurel? What have I got that you haven't?"

A bottle with the apothecary's seal on it, was what he had. The potion in it might work better, he said, than the same thing pulled out of the cupboard at home.

I thanked him and went home by way of Lynn Hall.

Snow on the fields was churned by tracks of horses and sleighs, but I heard no voices; the searchers had gone deep into the wood. The hall was silent and bitterly cold. Except for the dead, nothing had been touched. Candles and shards of glass still littered the floor; the frozen splash of blood shadowed the white marble. I paced on broken glass, shivering and trying to see through stone, to make it shift under my eyes into another world. I could see nothing beyond this one. The tapestry between the rooms caught at my attention, its pale, glittering threads suggesting patterns, landscapes, faces, that you could only glimpse out of the corner of your eye; they vanished into formlessness when you looked at them. I stared at it for a long time, trying to see into it, beyond it, to the place where I last saw it hanging above the mantel. Finally, impatiently, I pushed it aside.

She was there, waiting, in her winter wood. Her head swiveled on her shoulders like an owl's and I froze, stunned by the eerie movement. Her eyes caught mine; I felt my bones change shape. I was the mouse in the shadow of the owl's wing; I was snow drifting to her winds.

Come, they said, *come,* the winds that harvested dead leaves and froze the birds in flight. *Come with us. You belong with us.*

I could barely remember a human language. My lips were made of ice; they spoke ice instead of sound. *Corbet* formed between us, a glittering question.

He is waiting, her winds answered. *Come.*

I felt them pull at me, felt myself fray into them. But they had not told me if he was among her living or her dead. I pulled my bones out of the snow, shrugged my skin back over them, and saw her again, wild and beautiful, with her feral, dangerous smile, and her eyes like midsummer night.

"I want to see him." Even human, I could barely speak; words chattered piecemeal out of me. "I want to talk to him."

Somewhere behind me a door opened. Wind snarled; a white owl flew into a pale shimmer of light. I saw pristine folds of linen, the empty washbasin that held nothing, not even dust.

I let the tapestry close, and turned. Snow fell lightly over me, burned away like falling stars. I recognized Perrin's voice before the white mist faded and he caught me and I could see his face.

"Rois!" He opened his cloak, tried to bundle me under it. "What are you doing back here? You're like ice—"

"I was looking—" I had to stop, shudder something colder than the air out of me: the splinter of ice, maybe, that she had left in my heart. "I was looking for something—"

"Laurel went all through this place," he said grimly. "She didn't find a word. Can you drive home alone? Or shall I take you back?"

"I'll drive. I'm all right. What are you doing here?"

"Searching the wood. I saw your sleigh."

"Has anyone found anything?"

"Just more snow." His mouth tightened, holding back words. I saw the sudden bleakness in his eyes and wondered what he hoped to find: a body for Laurel to grieve over, or a silence that would haunt them for the rest of their lives. "And more of that on its way," he added finally, "just so things won't be too easy for us." He paused, his eyes straying over the scraps of story we were left with: the broken glass, the bloody hearth. I felt a shiver run through him, as if she had laid an icy finger on him. "It happened all over again," he breathed. "If you think about it the wrong way. Best get home, girl, before you freeze here and start haunting this place along with Nial Lynn."

I gave Laurel a stiff dose of the apothecary's potion that night, but still I fell asleep to her soft weeping. I found Corbet in my dreams, not where he might be, but in a time and place I wished we could return to. He stood again in that golden fall of summer light beside the rose vines, a slightly darker shade of gold, barely formed yet, something mysterious happening in a streak of sunlight that you would miss if you glanced at it and away, and not back again. The scent of roses hung in the still air, sweet and heavy, slowing time until summer seemed to stop, even in my dream, just at that moment: when I knew he was coming but just before I saw his face.

I woke in the dark with tears on my face, still smelling roses. I heard winter howling across the fields, singing in the eaves, casting some incomprehensible enchantment around the house. Down the hall, both Beda and my father snored, one frugally, fussily, the other in explosive, brandy-soaked mutterings. Through all that, one faint sound stopped my heart: Laurel, awake or weeping in her dreams for Corbet.

By morning we were cut off from the world; not even gossip could reach us. I stayed close to the fire with Laurel. Our father, shovelling out the cow stalls, came in for an occasional mouthful of brandy against the cold. He smelled of cows and wind; he molted snow as he stood at the fire, great crusts that he kicked into the hearth with boots tufted with frozen, dirty snow. Each time he came in, he would cast an absent glance at Laurel, worried without knowing it. She would lift the linen in her fingers and add a stitch. Each time he went out, she would let her sewing fall and stare out the window. Her face seemed calm, despite her swollen eyes, but it was pale as whey, and she had eaten almost nothing. I had no idea what she was making; neither, I suspected, did she.

I watched for owls in the snow-streaked wind. Laurel watched for Corbet. Sometimes memories formed out of the snow instead of owls. I would see Tearle's face untouched by time, see myself standing with Corbet in his father's dream of Lynn Hall, and I would feel a spidery chill of fear and wonder glide over me, that I had gone so far out of the human world and come back. *She has our eyes*, Tearle had said. *She has our eyes. She must have inherited them from someone*. Wordless questions clamored in me; I did not know what to ask, or what Laurel knew, or if there was anything at all to know.

As if she felt all my thoughts crowding around her,

Laurel stirred and turned from the window. She startled me, seeing me, it seemed, for the first time in two days. She picked up her sewing; for a moment she looked almost perplexed by it. Then she let it drop again. But her eyes went back to me instead of the snow, and she spoke without being spoken to, surprising me again.

"You're looking better. I worried for a while . . ." Her voice trailed.

I asked, to keep her talking, "Worried about what?"

The faint frown came and went between her brows; she answered softly, "I was thinking of our mother. You look so like her."

I stared at her, wondering if I had spoken aloud without realizing it. Then an ember flared suddenly, briefly, behind my eyes. "You thought—"

"Winter came, and she just stopped eating. She grew so thin. She would never say why. I would bring her things to eat—an apple, a cake—and she would smile at me and touch my hair and tell me how good I was." She looked down at her hands, found cloth there, and produced a stitch, pale thread on pale linen. I watched her, mute, my own hands so tightly linked I could feel only bone. "Later, I would hear Beda complain about finding rock-hard cakes beneath the cushions."

I saw Laurel then, as a child, with those great grey eyes, watching the terrible and incomprehensible thing she could not stop. "I was so little—I forgot how you—how much—"

"I forgot, too," she said simply. "Until you began to look too much like her."

"I'm sorry," I whispered, and expression, quick and formless, wind over water, passed across her face.

"It was a long time ago."

"Maybe. But now I'm old enough to know what I missed. Not having her. I had you instead. I never questioned that. I never thought how hard that must have been for you sometimes."

Her needle flashed, dropped, too heavy. "I never thought about it either. It was just something that needed to be done. Like most things around here. And there was always Beda to help."

"Tell me about her," I pleaded. "You all say I look like her, and yet all I know about her are sad things."

"I don't—I've hardly spoken of her for so many years." She was silent a little, then added helplessly, "It's your face that stirs up memories. Sometimes I look at you and I become the child I was then, just for an instant, and I remember things. The old ballads she played on the flute. Picking berries with her, in the brambles along the edge of the pasture on a hot day. How bees as fat as blackberries droned around us in the light, and she taught me words to songs while I dropped berries in my bucket. How a trip to the cobbler to measure my feet would take an afternoon; everyone stopped her to talk. She kept things tidy; she always had flowers in the house. Wildflowers from the wood, if nothing else . . ."

I hesitated, tried to ask one question by asking another. "Did—was she still happy after I was born? Was that when she changed?"

"No." Expression melted briefly through Laurel's

eyes. "She loved you. And I loved what she loved. She taught me to gather eggs while she held you, and embroider, and grow herbs . . ."

"She was happy," I said, oddly surprised. "No one ever told me that."

Laurel's face grew still again, indrawn. "I think we forgot," she said finally. "She was happy until that winter, and winter is what we remembered."

"What happened to her?" I touched Laurel's wrist when she didn't answer. "What do you think it was?"

She raised her eyes from her hands, stared into the fire. "They never knew. She had no fever, no pain. She just . . . did not live." She spoke silently then, looking at me. I stared at her thin, haunted face, her eyes that reflected all the emptiness she saw, and a sudden terror filled me because I didn't know which of us she had told her memories to, which of us she warned.

I heard my voice from far away, clear and steady, giving her words like a charm to keep her safe: "I have no intention of dying."

But she only answered, pulling the thread straight in another random stitch, "Neither did our mother. She just forgot to live."

In my dreams that night, I ran into the wild autumn wood. I heard the endless sigh of dying leaves, felt the tumultuous winds, the restless twilight riders. I found the rose vines and crouched beside them, making myself small, small, but still she saw me. Moonlight spilled from her eyes; the starry sky flowed behind her in her hair. I heard the silvery laughter of tiny bells. She bent toward me as I tried to bury myself in leaves. Gold dropped from her fingers. It glowed brighter and brighter as it fell between us, until in its rich light I saw her face.

I woke, still staring into darkness.

She wore my face.

Eighteen

The sudden storm had gone its way by dawn. Snow still fell, but fitfully; winds muttered now instead of shrieking. Waking, I wished I could understand their broken incantations. They knew something I needed to know; they teased and hinted, but they would not tell. I pulled a quilt over my shoulders and looked out the window. In the yard, my father had finished shovelling; he ran a rope down his path from the house to the barn, as if he were anchoring us to earth between storms. Along the road, sleigh runners had veered close to our gate, left their tracks in the new snow.

I heard the door open below. My father clumped in; wood clattered into the wood box. I went down, found him feeding the fire.

"Who was here?"

"Perrin stopped to leave some of his beer and ask

about Laurel. That's a good sign, isn't it?" he said hopefully.

"It's a sign of something," I agreed. "Did he bring any news with the beer?"

"Nothing new. No one has appeared looking for the stranger, and Corbet is still missing. Perrin said they'll search again today, when the snow stops." He paused, scratching one brow with his thumbnail. "He won't be still alive, if they do find him in a snowdrift. And if they don't—"

"I'm going to help look for him," I said abruptly. "No one knows the wood better than I do."

"Not the winter wood," he protested. "You never go into it."

"It's better than both of us staring out the window watching for him."

He tossed a log with unnecessary force onto the fire, but refrained from saying what he was thinking about our taste. "He's either frozen in a ditch along the road, or safely doing whatever business he left home for. Let them look. Stay with Laurel."

"She'll be better when he's found," I said without conviction. "And I can't stand being inside waiting."

He grumbled something dourly. But he couldn't really imagine me staying out long among the bleak, pinched faces of the winter trees. He changed the subject, hoping that, ignored, it would go away. "Perrin says a couple of them—Furl Gett and Travers' son, Willom—might be sent to the next township to find someone who knows how to look into these things. Some say it's village business, and we don't need to go digging up old trouble, curses and murders, and faces out of the past, for strangers to peer at. But we do have a dead body on our hands to deal with somehow." His eyes slid to me; he added tentatively, "It's you they'd question first, if we bring strangers into this."

"I know." I stared at the fire, thinking of two tales, one simple, one beyond comprehension, both peculiar. *I walked through a storm and fell asleep in an empty house; when I woke there was a dead man beside me.* . . . I heard the stairs creak, and turned to see Laurel drift down, dressed for the day, but not seeing it, her eyes already moving past us to the window.

She unnerved our father; he lost his temper suddenly, for no other reason, I knew, than to change the expression on her face.

"Stop watching for him. Whether or not he's alive, he's still a man with a cursed past and a fresh bloodstain on his floor. Look at you. He's not good for you. Swallow your pride and go find Perrin."

She turned to him; but for that it seemed she might not have heard him. "Perrin," she said, with faint surprise, as if Perrin were someone she had known in childhood and had long outgrown. I saw the blood rise in our father's face, the confusion in his eyes.

"The one you made all that lace for," he reminded her. "The one who still loves you, and would marry you if you stop chewing your heart up over a dream of Lynn Hall. That's all it ever was—only a daydream. Nothing solid. Nothing real, to start a life with."

"You don't know," she said softly. "You don't know

what there was between us. Perrin saw it, but you never did."

"Perrin said—"

"Perrin." She said the name without impatience, with an indifference far more chilling. "He'll forget about me. Corbet will return. He can't forget what we meant to each other."

Our father stared at her. "Over a supper or two? A glass or two of wine?"

"That's all you saw." She turned away from him to the dead world beyond the window. "That's all you ever saw."

"I don't know anymore what I saw," he admitted heavily, "but I don't like what I'm seeing now. It's too much to ask Rois to have any kind of common sense in winter, but you've always been the steady one. Stop grieving over a man who, alive or dead, left you without a word. Eat your breakfast, get your boots on, and go bring Perrin back. He'll play the flute and put some color into your face."

She did not bother to answer. He grumped back out to find some common sense among the cows. Laurel turned to me then, despair welling under the icy calm in her face.

"That's not why he left, is it?" she pleaded. "You didn't dream that, did you? He is not cursed, and he had nothing to do with the death of the stranger in his house. Tell me you don't believe that."

"No."

"And that wasn't all there was between us? Just a

glass or two of wine? Just a way to pass the winter hours? The master of Lynn Hall dallying with the farmer's daughters, making a little trouble to idle away the time?"

I shook my head, swallowing. "That's not what I saw."

"Then where is he?" she whispered and turned back to the window.

She sat down to breakfast later to please our father. I watched her push her spoon around a bowl of oatmeal, pull bread apart, lift milk to her lips and put it down, making all the small, constant gestures of eating, but never quite doing it. At first I thought our father did not notice. Then I realized that because it was Laurel, who didn't fall into rose vines or chase after winds, he thought he knew what to expect: She would find her way back.

But he did not realize how far she had already gone. I glimpsed it later in the embroidery she was doing: the patternless stitch of white on white, like footprints in snow that wandered randomly and went nowhere, crossing and circling themselves until they could not be followed.

The search party crossed the fields in the early afternoon, looking like bears in their winter furs and hoods. The wind was still now; nothing in the pale sky threatened. I did not dare ask my father for the sleigh. I pulled on high fur boots and walked the tumbled snow that a couple of the sleighs had made following the path from Lynn Hall that Corbet might have taken to reach the road. By then the searchers had all dispersed into the wood, or farther up the road. I saw one or two on snowshoes, tramping through the trees, kicking at drifts and peering up into the bare branches as if they expected to see Corbet there. By the time I reached the wood, they had all disappeared.

Others had been where I went; their snowshoes told me. Tracks passed all around the snow-covered vines; someone had kicked at the smooth mound of snow, found only briers instead of Corbet, and gone on. But they didn't know where to look, or how to see. I thought I did. Doors, he had said. Thresholds. Places of passage, where gold fell from one story into another, where time shifted across the boundary between worlds.

I had nowhere else to look.

I dug into the snow around the vines until they sprang loose and I could push them away from the well. Some, caught in ice, hung down like bars around the water. I couldn't break the ice with my hands. It was thick but oddly clear, like glass flecked with fine crystal stars, neatly fitted over the dark water. The spring was still now, frozen, I guessed, at the source.

The third time I called his name, he came to me.

I felt the painful shock of blood all through me, at the unexpected sight: his face, remote as a dream, gazing up at me out of the dark water. He must be dead, I thought wildly; he looked, trapped beneath the ice, in too terrible a place for any human touch to reach him.

But I tried: I laid one hand flat on the ice, and his hand rose up through the cold to spread itself against mine. I could see so little of him—his face, his hair, his hand; the rest was brief, isolated needles of color flickering through the deep water.

Tears rolled down my face, froze as they fell, and scattered like tiny pearls across the ice.

"Corbet," I whispered. "Are you dead?"

His voice seemed to come from a place that far. "No."

"Can you come out of the well?"

"This is as close as I can come to you. Rois, how did you know to look for me here?"

"I found you here before," I said numbly. "I can see you in water, I can see you in light. I don't know how. And I don't know how to reach you. If I break the ice—"

"You can't break into her world with a stone. You know that." Beneath the ice, his eyes reflected winter greys and shadows; I had to remember green. "Rois, leave me here."

"No."

"She killed my father." The expression frozen on his face splintered; his face twisted, and I saw a sudden flash of color. "He fought for me."

"I know." My hand pushed against the ice, as if wishing could warm and melt it, as if his face would be there when I touched water. "She left him in this world. I found him on the hearth beside me when I woke."

He made a soft, anguished sound, as if he suddenly felt the burning cold. "She left him there? In those two rooms?"

"He still—he looks as he did in your world. Her world. The oldest villagers say they recognize him."

He closed his eyes. "She still holds him spellbound."

"They're searching for you. You vanished, just like your father, leaving a dead man in your house."

"Nial Lynn's curse." He looked at me again, his eyes heavy, bitter. "She left me that to come back to, if I leave her. Do they think I killed him?"

"No one knows what to think."

"It doesn't matter. I might as well have killed him; I forced her to."

"No—"

"We would still be with him, you and I, and he would be alive if he hadn't fought her. She knows you now. If I make promises to her, she might leave you in peace."

"What kind of promises?" I asked. He hesitated, choosing words. I found them for him. "To stay with her always? To forget that you ever tried to become human, or that your father died trying to set you free? She might leave me in peace, but you won't, because I will look for you in every fall of light. I will come there for you."

"Rois," he breathed. "Don't say that in this place."

"You may never find your way back into this world if I don't. How will I explain that to Laurel?"

His face grew still, luminous in the dark water. "Laurel."

"She stands at the window waiting for you. She won't eat, she weeps at night, she barely remembers who Perrin is. It's as if she's under a spell, only what she knows and wants is no longer love but sorrow."

He was silent, staring up at me; I wondered for a moment if she had turned him into his own reflection.

Then I saw him shudder. "It's my fault. I tried to love in human ways—that's what Laurel expected. I pretended to be what she wanted, what she thought I was. I lied too well."

My hand closed around cold; I was shaking, but if I moved my hand from the ice, he might vanish. "You lied to both of us. I believed you—"

"You saw me." His voice sounded suddenly harsh with pain. "I could never pretend to you—you saw me too well."

"I don't know what I saw. I thought I knew what you were, who I was, but you changed under my eyes, and so has Laurel and so has the wood, and I don't know anymore what I am except a woman who sees too much."

"I know. I always knew."

"What did you always know?"

"That you see with the wood's eyes."

I had to swallow fire before I could speak. One hand outstretched to him seemed the only thing I recognized of myself; the rest of me seemed so far from human that no one I knew would know me anymore. "So you see—" I had to begin again. "So you see why I can't leave you here. Why I can't walk away from you. You are my shadow, the one thing I can't run fast enough in the human world to escape. You knew me before I knew myself." My hand opened again beside his face. "I need you."

"You must be careful," he whispered. "You must be so careful. Even need is a path to her."

"I know. But if I turn away from you, where will I go to find Laurel? Tell me how to be careful. Tell me how not to see what my heart sees. Tell me how to live without you both."

He was silent; I saw him gather breath and loose it, in a pearly mist that filled the water and flowed around him until I could barely see his hand, still reaching out to mine against the ice. "Corbet," I cried, and felt the cold, as if the mist had seeped into my bones. I turned suddenly, as it touched my heart; a brier seized my hood, another clung to my shoulder.

"Rois," she said. She wore glittering air and spindrift snow, and a mantle made of tiny living animals in their winter white. She stroked one or two, smiling; their eyes were wide and terrified, their crying voices mute. "I know what your heart sees. I will show you."

"Who are you?" I whispered. Cold racked through me; the thorns tightened their hold. She was something wild in my wood, the glint of an eye on a lightless night, the formless shadow the moon reveals tangled in the shadow of a tree. "Who are you?"

"I am night," she said, and it was. "I am winter's song," and I heard it. "I am the shadow of the bloody moon and all the winds that harvest in it." I felt them. "I am the dead of winter."

She wore my mother's face.

Nineteen

Salish and Furl Gett and Willom Travers found me stumbling through the trees, and gave me a ride home. Packed in the sleigh among fumes of beer and wet wool, I watched the dark wood slowly close around itself behind us, hiding its secrets. The searchers, frustrated, perplexed, passing the last of the beer among them, tried to piece together a tale from scraps.

It was Corbet Lynn's brother, with their father's face and their grandfather's evil ways, who had come to force a quarrel with Corbet over his inheritance.

It was just some stranger who had lost his horse and his way, who crawled in to escape the storm and collapsed beside the dying embers.

Corbet Lynn was Nial Lynn reborn—you could see it in his face—and the stranger on his hearth was an innocent relation who had the bad luck to wear something resembling Tearle's face into Lynn Hall on the night of the curse.

Corbet Lynn was a generous man who couldn't slap a gnat without remorse—look how he helped Crispin and Aleria—and the stranger wandering in from the cold had betrayed Corbet's kindness by dropping dead in his house while he was away.

Both Corbet and the stranger were ghosts—look how they came out of nowhere and had no ties—who had roused out of their graves on the eve of the curse, and this time Nial had gotten revenge on his son after a raging brawl that overturned all the candlesticks in the house.

Corbet had left just before the storm, on business matters, and he was ignorant as a fence post about what he was going to find on his plate when he got home.

Corbet Lynn was a man cursed from the day he was born to repeat his father's murder and vanish like his father, and it was the stranger's misfortune to turn up at Corbet's door on that fateful winter night.

"Corbet wouldn't kill anyone," Salish insisted. "Even if he was cursed. Anyway, Rois said Corbet was never even there."

"Rois was asleep," Willom argued, wanting violence and mystery to wile away the winter.

"She wouldn't sleep through a murder. Not if they were breaking things around her. What do you think, Rois? You're his neighbor. You know him."

"The stranger died of cold," I said shortly. I could barely think, even to rescue Corbet's reputation. "Blane said that may be true. Corbet went away on business and he can't get back because of weather."

They looked at one another and at me, unconvinced. *You know something,* their eyes said to me. *Nobody could sleep through that.* Willom shook his head, turning the sleigh into our yard.

"Why was the stranger dressed like that? Like he'd come to stay, not just appeared at the door? Why did Corbet leave his house and his stable open unless he left too fast to bother about them and he wasn't coming back? And why does the stranger look like Corbet's father?"

"Nobody knows that except our grannies," Furl Gett said. He corked the beer and pulled me out of the jumble of fur and snowshoes. "And they just see to suit themselves. Truth is, we don't know what we're looking for, or what we'll find under the snow. There's something buried there, though, if nothing but a dead horse. There's something hidden."

My father grumbled at me when I walked in; Laurel picked the despair out of my expression and turned away.

"They didn't—" our father asked as I hung my cloak.

"No."

"Is there any—"

"No."

I sat close to the fire after supper, brooding and trying to warm the chill out of my heart. I kept seeing my mother's face, recognizing it, or thinking I did; maybe it was a lie, a reflection, my own face with a few subtle changes. I had seen such tricks before. But I could not stop thinking about my mother, and what she might have watched for, as Laurel watched now, during her last winter. She died longing for spring, our father said. If she had known the spring she wanted would return to her, she would have waited. But that last winter told her such a season would never come again, not to her in this world. So she had gone elsewhere.

How far, I wondered with bleak horror, had she gone?

"You're looking," our father said abruptly, picking thoughts out of my head, "more and more like your mother every day. Except that her expression was sweeter."

He was frowning again. Beside him, Laurel picked up the cup of tea I had made her, and took a bird's sip.

"You said I was unlike my mother." I felt the cold fear in my fingers, my face, but somehow I answered calmly. "That she never ran wild in the wood. She never would have gotten trapped in the roses. She wouldn't have even stayed out past twilight."

"True," he admitted. Somehow that did not comfort him. "But you did, so I'm never sure what you might do next. At least you're not lying weak and silent, gazing out a window for something that never comes."

I heard the unspoken words in his voice: *something I could not bring her, though I would have given her everything*. I gazed at him, at the familiar furrows and hillocks of his face, his round eyes the color of smoke, that saw simple things he put simple names to.

Am I your child? I asked him silently, urgently, my lips caught hard between my teeth so that the words would not break out. *Or am I the wood's*?

But he did not know how to hear such questions. He could not bring her spring, he thought, and so she died.

"Was there a name for it?" I asked softly, trying to keep my voice steady. "What she died of?"

He shook his head, his eyes on the fire, seeing memories. "The apothecary couldn't give a name to it. She did not seem to suffer. She told him something, though, that he didn't tell me until later. After. That she just did not feel comfortable in this world." He raised his eyes bewilderedly. "What other world did she want? What world did she dream of? You're like her there," he added accusingly. "You dream too much. You see too much into things; you get too close to them, make them into something else. Imagination." He pounced on the word with grim satisfaction. "You have too much of it. So does everyone around here in winter. Too much cold and too much beer. People start hearing curses, seeing ghosts."

"Something happened in Lynn Hall," Laurel said, startling us. She had turned her still eyes from the window to his face. "What do you think happened?"

He was silent, studying his pipe before he lit it. He said finally, "I think the whole task became too much for Corbet—rebuilding that old wreck. Winter brought him to his senses and he went back to wherever he came from. The stranger was just that; he was lost and half-frozen, and he died of natural causes, accidently spilling blood all over a murder half a century old. That's what I think." But he frowned uncertainly at the smoke he puffed. Laurel rose abruptly, her linen and needle sliding unheeded to the floor. I picked them up; she turned restively to a window, stared out at the wailing dark. I watched with her, listening to the ruthless wind that had called our mother's name, wondering if Laurel heard it, too.

That night I dreamed of Corbet trapped in the well. I couldn't break the ice between us, but my hand passed through it as if I were made of air, and he reached up through the deadly cold toward me. I gripped him, and as I drew our hands out of the ice I saw that winter had stripped our fingers bare; we held each other's bones.

Awake, I could not sit still, I could not think. When my father hitched the sleigh after breakfast to take Beda to the village, I pleaded with him to let me drive her. She wanted a day with her younger sister's family, she'd said, to gossip and cook a meal for those who would enjoy it instead of worrying it into crumbs. I would leave her at her sister's house, I promised my father, and make one stop at the apothecary's and then come home so quickly I would meet myself going. He didn't bother to ask me why I wanted to go to the apothecary's. If news of Corbet was anywhere to be had, it would be there.

But I didn't go there to talk about Corbet.

"You knew my mother," I said to Blane. "You tried to help her, that winter when she died."

He looked at me silently. His shop empty for the moment, he was mixing oil, rosewater and dried leaves for someone's cold. I smelled wintergreen and licorice. I had never thought about his age before; he had been in my life as long as I had. But as I watched his expression change, suddenly haunted by memories, I glimpsed the face my mother must have known. He was no older than my father, I realized. They had still been young then, watching their youth die slowly through the winter.

"Yes," he answered finally. "What is it, Rois? What did you come to ask me?"

"Why she died. No one seems to know." He waited, his hands still, until I gave him more. "Laurel and my father both say I look like her. I asked them both what she died of; they couldn't tell me. Winter. That's all my father knows. She died of winter. I don't remember her. I wish I did. They try to tell me about her; they try to answer my questions. But I don't understand the answers. People die of cold and sickness, they don't die from looking at a season."

His hands began to move again, measuring, grinding. "I don't know much more than that," he said slowly. "If I had been able to put a name to why she died, it would have spared me some grief. It was hard, not knowing how to help, not knowing why."

"Did she tell you anything?"

He looked back across the years again; I saw bewilderment and sorrow, but nothing hidden, nothing locked away behind his eyes. "She wanted some other place," he said finally, "that was not life. We don't have that many choices: We either have this world or not. She lost interest in it." He shook more leaves into his mortar. "It was some kind of sickness, of course it was. Maybe someone with more experience would have recognized it. But I had never seen it before, and I have never seen it since." He paused then, studying me. "You do look like her. Very much like her. No wonder you stir up memories. I wish I had a better answer. I had just begun to work on my own then; my father had taken to his bed and left everything to me. I hadn't learned yet that I didn't have a remedy for everything. I didn't have a remedy for life."

Tears of sorrow and frustration burned behind my

eyes, because I never knew her, because no one ever had. I forced them back. "Thank you."

He shook his head without looking at me. "How's Laurel?"

"No worse."

He looked at me then. "But no better." He straightened, perhaps to suggest something; the door opened abruptly. Crispin, none the worse for marriage, fatherhood or the weather, came in trailing whiffs of pipe smoke and beer. He gave me the sweet, generous smile he still gave to every woman who hadn't yet lost her second set of teeth.

"Rois."

Blane reached for a jar, poured a simmering concoction into it. "Tell your grandfather to follow this with tea, not brandy. Have they solved our murder yet at the inn?"

Crispin's smile faded, left a line between his fair brows. "We were trying to remember . . ." he said, then stood a moment trying to remember what it was they had been trying to remember. "Oh. Where it was Corbet said he lived before he came here. Do you know?"

"I never asked him," Blane said.

"Nobody did, it seems. But somebody must have. It's one of the things everyone thought they knew until they were asked. He must have told someone." Crispin turned to me hopefully. "Rois. You'd know. You were neighbors."

"He never said."

"You mean you never asked?"

"We might have. I don't remember that he answered. You saw him more than anyone—"

"I thought I knew," he answered simply. "I thought we all knew."

"The way we all knew his father was dead," I said without thinking.

He only looked at me blankly. "He is dead. That's why Corbet came here. Nobody," he added a trifle challengingly to the apothecary, "can tell me that Corbet Lynn killed anyone anywhere for any reason. I worked with him, I knew him—"

Blane interrupted patiently. "Someone's going to look for him in the place where he came from? Is that it?"

"Yes." He blinked at Blane a moment. "Yes. Except that nobody can lay a finger on exactly where . . ."

Blane melted wax on the jar and set his seal into it. "It's a good idea, though."

"It is," Crispin agreed. "I thought of it. And I'll go, no matter the weather, the moment anyone remembers. He was kind to us, Aleria and me. I don't believe he killed anyone, I don't believe he's dead in a ditch, and I don't believe that Nial Lynn's ghost had anything to do with it."

The apothecary's brows flickered. He passed the jar to Crispin and added his grandfather's name to a list of unfinished business. "What do you believe?" he asked curiously. I listened for the answer, too. But Crispin did not seem to know.

"He was called away suddenly. And then this stranger happened into his house wanting shelter from the storm . . ."

The stranger from nowhere without a horse . . . I

turned to Blane, who was busying himself with his pestle. "Thank you," I said again. He frowned slightly, absently, as at an old and familiar ache.

"Come and visit me again," he said. "Let me know how Laurel is."

"I will. Goodbye, Crispin."

That smile broke through him again, like sun through cloud, that warms you while it has nothing to do with you at all. Then he dropped the jar into his pocket and leaned over the counter. "Anyway—the stranger is nearly dead with cold, and he sees Rois' dying fire . . ."

I closed the door.

I saw her then, standing still as a tree with a white owl on her shoulder, where the sheep grazed in fairer seasons on the green. She wore a mantle of white feathers that covered her from throat to heel. Only her hair flowed freely around her, blown by winds no human could feel on that dead calm morning.

Her eyes were closed. The owl opened its eyes and looked at me. Its eyes were as gold as the sun I could only see in memory.

It asked its familiar question.

I closed my eyes. "I do not know," I heard myself whisper. "You tell me."

When I opened my eyes again, there was only a tree standing in the snow, a white owl sleeping in the dark, airy swirl of its branches.

Twenty

I shaped her out of every drift of snow as I drove home; I wished her out of air and cloud to come to me and guide the sturdy, placid plow horses beyond the boundaries of this world, to the place where roses opened beneath water and white owls spoke with human voices. There she would tell me what no one else seemed to know. But because I wanted her, she did not come; the horses followed their own tracks home and turned into the yard.

I saw my father there, reshaping his frozen, dirty path to the barn, paring it close to the ground before the next storm. I unhitched the horses, but left the sleigh out for my father to bring Beda home later. When I put the horses in their stalls and turned, I saw him again, framed in the open barn door. He leaned on the shovel, puffing tiredly. Beyond him Laurel stood at the window, watching the distant fields.

I closed my eyes, pushed my hands against them, against the fears swooping and screeching like rooks through my head. I couldn't face the silence in that house, the loneliness that Laurel left behind her as she went her way without us. I did not know what to do for any of us, except find another shovel hanging on a nail and start whittling up my father's path to meet him.

He stopped a moment, shocked to find me working. I was not a great deal of help; though I tried, I couldn't shovel my way beyond the world, or even beyond my own thoughts. But my father didn't comment. As he drew closer to me, I heard his faint, breathy whistling.

Our paths met finally, mine not far from the barn. He leaned on his shovel again, watching me pant.

"What possessed you?" he asked mildly, a fair question since I had only a vague idea which end of a snow shovel was up. I shrugged, evading his eyes.

"You looked tired," I said.

"I was," he admitted. He reached out, tucked a strand of my hair back into my hood, awkwardly, with his blunt, gloved hand. "Odd how much better you can work with someone helping. I didn't expect you back yet. I thought you'd go off somewhere looking for Corbet, or messages, or roses, something."

I shook my head. "I've run out of places to look."

"No news in the village?"

"No."

He frowned, reaching out to give my shoulder a

vague, comforting pat. "Strange. You'd think someone would be searching at their end for the dead . . ." His voice trailed; he was staring suddenly at Laurel in the window. I saw his hands tighten on the shovel, heard his startled breath. He murmured something I didn't catch; perhaps he was laying his own curse on Nial Lynn.

But that wasn't the ghost in his head. "For a moment I saw your mother," he said huskily. "The way your sister stands there . . . At least with Laurel, I know what she's watching for. I wish she'd pull herself out of it. Should I get Perrin over here? Would that help her?"

"I don't know." I felt the cold then, seeping up out of the ground into my bones. "She might only hurt him again."

"She might be missing him without knowing it."

I doubted it. "Maybe."

"She can't go on like this. Brooding out at the winter, not eating." He brooded at her for a breath or two, then reached out, still watching her, to take my shovel. "She looks like—she's doing what—" But he couldn't say it. His mouth tightened; he hefted the shovels under his arm. "I'll give her a day or two," he muttered. "But no more. Not the entire winter."

Still he lingered; he shifted, chilled, but he could not seem to turn away from Laurel. He was looking through her at his own past, I knew, and I could not say anything to comfort him; I could only stand frozen in the snow, terrified of what he might find there.

I touched him finally, and he looked at me, an expression on his face that I had never seen before. He didn't recognize me in that moment. He gave me a stranger's blank, impersonal stare, as if he did not know whose child I was, or where I had wandered from into his life. He turned and walked away from me into the barn.

I waited, shivering, blinking back tears, unable to move, wondering if I still had a name, a home, a father, or if he had seen what I must be, and had left me orphaned in his heart. He came back out in a moment, closed the barn door, and suddenly his face was familiar again: kindly, stubborn, perplexed.

"Thank you, Rois. Now get in before you freeze."

I dreamed that night of gold falling from a slender hand, gold turning brighter and brighter as it fell, until it blazed like the sun in the night. Someone dropped the gold; someone else watched it fall. I saw no faces, but in the dream I knew that I dropped the gold, I watched it fall. . . .

The wind spoke to me just before I woke.

I understood it in that instant, all its wild songs, its mutterings and shriekings, its warnings. *Gold*, it said, so clearly that I carried the word out of dreams into morning. *Gold*, I told myself as I opened my eyes, clinging to the word as fiercely as if it were the answer to all the wind's enchantments, the word to free us from our spellbound world.

But gold turned to nothing in the chill grey dawn; the world remained unchanged. Laurel drifted like a moth, silent and colorless, from window to window. Sometimes I stood with her, trying to see Lynn Hall within the trees. If I chose to go, winter would meet me there, she would take me into her heart, show me what I wanted to know. She had dropped the gold, she had watched it fall . . . But if I left this house I might never return to it, I thought starkly. I might see too much, see in a way that changed everything I knew. Even Corbet might be transformed in my eyes, in my heart. I would be trapped, like him, between worlds . . . My thoughts crossed the fields again and again; I lingered beside Laurel, silent and afraid, while searchers appeared and disappeared around Lynn Hall, the only movement in the world.

Perrin rode over that afternoon. I didn't know if our father had sent a message to him, or if, in the charmed way of lovers, he had heard her name coupled with his, and had put down his axe or his leather needle to come to her. Laurel saw him out the window, so his knock at the door did not present her with a moment of mystery or hope. She turned to sit, picked up her strange embroidery without a flicker of interest, as if he were Salish come to deliver a dozen bottles of wine from the inn. I opened the door. Perrin gave me a brief smile, his face, with its winter pallor, becoming suddenly whiter as he saw Laurel.

She had grown thinner, colorless, her movements random and without energy. But the remoteness in her eyes, as if we were all barely visible, as if she could not remember that she had ever kissed Perrin or why, was most disturbing. I felt the shock that ran through Perrin; for an instant he could not move or breathe. I saw her through his eyes then, and the same thought snapped through the troubled air around him into me: Her eyes looked already dead.

I am the dead of winter.

"Laurel," he breathed, fumbling with his cloak ties; he aimed the cloak at a peg and it fell into a damp heap on the floor. He went to her. I hung up his cloak and, too restless to sit still, I left them alone and went into the kitchen to chop onions for Beda's stew.

Beda fussed around me; what trouble she thought I could bring on myself with a knife and an onion, I couldn't imagine. I was too busy listening through her anxious flutterings for other voices. After a while I heard the stairs creak. I did not hear the front door close. I made a cup of tea and took it to Perrin, who was alone, staring into the fire. I said his name. He started, then leaned down to heave a log into the lagging flames.

I gave him the tea; he took a swallow and some color fanned into his face. He looked into the cup and grimaced.

"What is this?"

"Camomile."

"I thought it was beer." He set the cup on the mantel and looked at me, his eyes still stunned. "All that," he said unsteadily, "over Corbet Lynn. I wish I knew how he did it. There must have been some moment when I could have stepped between them and changed things. When I should have talked instead of playing the flute, or played instead of talking, or talked of love instead of cows—It's like swimming down a river and suddenly finding it changed its course and ran somewhere without you, stranding you in mud and stones, leaving you wondering what happened, where all the deep, sweet water went." Wood kindled and snapped; he added, staring at it, "I'd like to murder Corbet Lynn. If he's not already dead."

That aspect had not occurred to me. "It's not that simple," I protested.

"Then what is it, if it's not that simple? He trifled with her feelings and who knows what else? It was just a game to him, seeing if he could take what she was giving someone else. And when he got her attention and her heart, he got bored with her and—

"Killed someone and left her."

"I could bear it better if he had been honest. If he were here now instead of me. But disappearing like that, no message, no farewell, nothing, just leaving her like that—"

"Without a word, a message, a farewell to anyone, he got on his horse and rode away in the middle of the worst storm we've ever seen? Because he was bored?"

"You were there, Rois." He caught me with his clear, angry eyes, held me. "You were there. You dreamed yourself there, you said, and went back to sleep, then woke to find a dead man beside you. You've been digging up curses all winter; you've been watching Corbet, expecting some disaster. I think you're protecting him. Maybe you don't know where he is, but I think you know what happened at Lynn Hall that night and why a stranger died there. I don't think you closed your eyes to anything."

He was near, but as far from the truth as any of us. "I didn't see him die," I said wearily. "If I had, do you think I could have fallen asleep beside him? And I've been out searching the wood for Corbet, too."

"Did you see the stranger before he died? Was Corbet there when he came in?"

"No," I answered to the second question; the first he wouldn't want to know. He hesitated, perplexed and unconvinced; I veered away from the subject. "Corbet has been here for months, getting to know us, giving people work, even getting Crispin to work. There's no one who didn't like him—"

"I could have lived without him," Perrin said testily. "Maybe the stranger could have, too."

"So you believe he was a stranger?"

"Well, he's not Tearle Lynn, still looking like that after fifty years—"

"And you think Corbet killed him?"

"Not if he was a stranger, blowing in from the cold. If he was a brother, or a cousin, or something, then maybe Corbet had some reason."

"To leave the body there beside me where the whole village could know about it? Why didn't he just hide it and send me home to bed?"

"I don't know."

"Or at least wash the blood off his hands and write Laurel a love letter promising to return after a few years when the fuss died down."

He was silent, his mouth tight. He picked up the poker, struck a swarm of sparks out of a log. "I don't know." He dropped the poker then, sighing. "It's such a tangled mess, all those old tales we imagined colliding with what we know is true. And Laurel in the middle, caught between tale and truth. Sometimes I think he must be dead, and that's what she really sees when she stares out the window: that he's never coming back."

I frowned at the fire, my fingers closing tightly on my arms. "Our father thinks she is doing what our mother did. Wasting away in winter because she could not—she could not remember how to live. Or why."

He dropped a hand on my shoulder. "I remember that time," he said gently. "A little. I remember sitting with Laurel once under the grape vines. She wouldn't come out and she wouldn't say what was wrong. And then I simply stopped seeing your mother. They tried to explain it to me, but it took me some time to believe that death didn't stay in the fields or the barn with the animals, it could come into the house." I felt his hand shift, heard him hesitate before he spoke again. "I never understood what ailed your mother."

"Neither did my father."

His hand tightened abruptly, finding bone, before he let go of me. I looked at him; he was gazing blindly at the fire, his brows knit, his mouth a thin line. Even animals, I thought numbly, did that sometimes: wasted away for someone, something, that never returned to them. I heard Perrin draw a breath unsteadily. He met my eyes finally, his own eyes shocked, bewildered, trying to see who my mother might have watched for in the empty winter fields.

He said only, his voice catching, "You stay well, Rois. Laurel needs you."

"I will. And you'll come—"

"Yes. She won't care," he added with a touch of bitterness. "But I can't stay away. And maybe, if I keep coming back instead of him, she'll remember that once she cared."

He kissed my cheek and went to the door. I felt his eyes as he swung his cloak over his shoulders and tied it, as he opened the door. Did your mother? they asked. Did she watch the fields for someone? Who was he? Did he come like Corbet Lynn, a stranger riding in with summer to vanish in the winter? Or had they known each other longer? How long? You have her face. You are like her. You have your mother's eyes.

Where did you get your sight?

Who are you?

Who? the owl asked.

Gold fell from the sky through my thoughts and I remembered.

Twenty-one

Her face, looking down at me.

My face, which would become hers.

The gold that fell between us, turning, turning, in the summer light: the tiny circle in which I trapped wind-blown roses, leaves, flying birds, until she came back to me.

Her gold wedding ring.

My throat burned as if I had swallowed gold and it had stuck there, an O of astonishment. I stood stunned in the doorway, while Perrin rode away from me into winter, and in a world he did not see, the fields and barren wood turned to green and gold and shadow in the light of memory.

She must have carried me there secretly, perhaps while Laurel stayed with Beda and our father worked the distant fields. I smelled the roses as she laid me down, and the cool, mysterious scent of hidden water. She took off her wedding ring for me to play with, while she shaped longing into light, and light into the still, blurred figure waiting for her. She turned away from me, growing smaller and smaller until she met him in my ring of gold, and they both vanished into shadow.

She died trying to shape the barren light of memory into love.

"Rois." Laurel's voice, so infrequent now, startled me back into our world. I was still standing in the doorway, letting winter in. "It's cold." I moved and she shut the door behind me. She had been lying down, but her heavy eyes, the reflection of empty fields in them, told me she had not slept. "Is something wrong?"

Yes! I wanted to shout. I don't know whose bones I have, whose eyes. If my mother had a lover from the wood when I was already born, then who gave me my sight? Or did she know him long before I was born? Had I come to life in secret, in a hot fall of light on a summer day, an idea so inconceivable to anyone that not even my mother questioned who my father was? I turned away from Laurel's eyes, straightened a chair, and then a rug I had kicked askew, feeling my blood beat like tiny, frantic wings through me. I couldn't ask Laurel; she didn't know. No one human knew. She drifted to a window, but not even she could see, in the way our mother saw, past her human heart to what she loved.

After a while, she spoke again. "Rois, you're pacing."

I stopped. "I'm sorry."

"It's the season. You've always hated it. Everything one color, the coldest color of all."

Her voice chilled me. It had lost all its color, as if she could no longer see beyond white. "I need to do something," I said. All my pacing would only weave a web around itself; I couldn't walk out of the world. Laurel's attention strayed away from me, and again I felt the urgent, desperate wings. She had so little time to give me, and what time she had I was afraid to find my way out of. I had no choice; I said tightly, "I'm going to Lynn Hall."

"No one's there," Laurel said wearily. But she had turned away from her own reflection to look at me.

"Maybe he left some message we both missed."

"I looked. He left nothing."

"You were looking for words. There are other ways to leave a message."

Her eyes darkened, wandered past me then; she wanted simple answers, a message meant for her, not Rois' winter imaginings. She moved to the stairs, began to climb them, her steps slow and isolated, like an old woman's. "I suppose it might do you good to get out," she said with listless indifference. "But it's pointless going to Lynn Hall. He left nothing there for any of us."

Our father grumbled, but hitched the sleigh for me; even he was desperate for the straw that blew the direction Corbet had gone. "Everyone in the village has been in and out of that place for days. I don't know what you expect to find that they haven't. I want you back," he added, "before I remember that you're gone."

I left the sleigh in front of the hall and stepped into the twilight of an empty house. It was scarcely warmer inside. I left footprints across the threshold that did not melt. A corner of tapestry, or an edge of eyelet lace on a pillow, might have snapped like ice in my hand. Fire itself would have frozen on the grate. Others had been in here, left messages of one kind or another. Someone had written Corbet's name in ash on the marble mantel; there was a swallow of stale beer in one of his glasses. Boot prints had tracked around the stain in the hearthstones, drawn to it as if the curse itself lay there, silent yet dangerous, winter's unsolved mystery.

I knelt beside it, piled bits of half-charred wood left on the grate, and kindling someone had spilled carelessly on the floor. I was trying to build a fire without a flame, with only a wish to light it. I couldn't stay in that bitter cold, and I did not want to leave.

"Corbet," I whispered hopelessly, my hands to my mouth, warming my fingers with his name.

A rose bloomed on the grate and burst into flame.

The kindling caught and blazed, fire pouring out of the cold wood as if it had been trapped there, waiting to be freed. Through it the rose opened fiery petals, consuming but never consumed. I smelled both summer and winter in those flames: roses and the burning heart of applewood, the scent of wood in snow.

The stones began to burn.

I got to my feet then, backed away. Fire ate the hearth, the chimney stones, swarmed into the walls. Like a painting held too close to a taper, the room began to melt around me. I stood in the middle of it, staring at what the weaving and parting strands of fire revealed: colors I had never seen in winter, colors I had never seen together in one season, every shade of green.

I saw Corbet as the flames turned into gold. I stood on grass, feeling sunlight on my hair, my hands. I had not imagined any world he would have died to leave could be so beautiful. He stood beneath an oak tree; the ivy that wound up its trunk and through its branches trailed a tendril of green leaves to touch his hair. His eyes reflected a distant landscape. I said his name without sound. Something changed in his eyes then, light gilding a snow-bound field, revealing cold, concealing cold.

"Rois."

He lifted his hand to meet mine; this time light and air and invisible leaves separated us. I could hear them massed and rustling between us; he seemed as far from me as ever.

"Corbet, where are you?" I pleaded. "Where am I?"

His voice shook. "With me. Even here."

"But where?" Spring, I guessed, seeing a bank of purple violets spilling down into a rill. Then I saw burdock as high as my shoulder, and blue vervain, and yarrow the rich ocher-gold of late summer light. And then I saw leaves as golden as the yarrow.

The air smelled of violets, crushed raspberries, wood smoke. If I could have dreamed a world to escape the winter, I thought dazedly, it would be this timeless nowhere, in which green trembled like water, even in deep shadow, as if we stood at the bottom of a translucent pool.

"Is this where we came before?" I breathed. "The world you left to walk into my world?" I stopped, hearing myself. *My world,* I had said, drawing dangerous boundaries. *Your world.*

He smiled a thin, bitter smile I remembered. "It's one

of her faces. One of her expressions. You've seen others; don't lose your heart to this one."

"It's tempting." I tasted light on my lips as I spoke; a breeze shifted leaves and it filled my eyes. Corbet's face blurred against the ivy as if it were just emerging, shades of gold against the green, as I had first seen it. My hand, reaching out to him again, closed again on nothing. "What has she done to you? She has hidden you somewhere—"

"She has hidden me from you. She knows you're here. She knows why."

"Does she? Does she know I came here because I have no place else to go?"

"What do you mean?"

"No one else can tell me about my mother—no one else knows that my mother came into these woods in summer, where the rose vines fall across the secret well, and met someone in a fall of light—"

"How do you know?" he demanded.

"I remember."

"How do you know he was not human?"

"Because she watched for him," I whispered, "in winter, the way Laurel watches for you. She died waiting for him to return. I don't know myself any longer. I don't know where I belong. I can see my way here, so I must belong here. At least, when you look at me and say my name, I recognize myself."

"Why do you trust her?" he demanded recklessly. "You saw her heart—it's a howling desert of ice. She lies like the moon lies, a different face every night, all but one of them false, and the one true face as barren and hard as stone. Why do you believe her?"

"You do." My words came out ragged with unshed tears. "You knew me the moment you saw me. You said I see with the wood's eyes. That's why you turned to Laurel. You were afraid of me."

"Rois—" He was trembling; I could hear the leaves rustling around him. "Yes. You seemed to live in the borderlands of the world I tried to escape. You tossed your heart after every passing breeze. Even after light. You did not seem—"

The word pushed through my throat like two hard stones. "Human."

Unseen leaves whispered the word. He said slowly, "I never knew until now what that word could mean. Here in her world of dreams and deadly lies, you seem very human."

"Corbet." I swallowed something bitter. "Do you care for me at all? Or do you only need me?"

He breathed a word: yes, or no, or Rois. His hand opened to my face; I felt only the cool invisible leaves. I lifted my own hand; in the light our shadows touched.

"You come to me," he whispered. "Into every dark place. Into every memory. Into the empty eyes of winter. I go alone and find you with me. Why do you care for me?"

I did not know until I spoke. "Because you are making me human."

Again my hand found air and light, illusion, where my heart cried out for mortal flesh and bone. His face twisted as if he heard my cry. He looked down to where we could touch, and closed his eyes.

I heard her voice then, a memory in the sighing

leaves: *You must hold fast to him, no matter what shape he takes . . .*

"How can I hold light?" I demanded in despair.

You must love him.

"You cannot," he answered wearily.

You must be human to love.

I could hold him in my eyes, at least, for as long as she let him stay. "How much of you can she claim?" I asked him. "Some part of you is human."

"My father married just as Nial Lynn married: a woman who had strayed into an accidental smile in his eyes. She could not escape this place once she desired it. He tried. He tried to love her. But he had never been taught how."

"Then you don't belong here at all—"

"Long ago a mortal man went walking in the summer wood one day near Lynn Hall. He fell in love with a stir of air, a scent of wild roses, a touch of light. She bore him a son."

"Nial Lynn."

He nodded. "My great-grandfather's human wife took the child to raise, but she was not pleased with him. Nial had strange powers, and was prone to odd fits of violence. But they had no other children. So he inherited Lynn Hall. I think he must have hated the human world because he could not find his way past it into her world."

"Why didn't she—"

He smiled a little, tightly. "Because he wanted it. She only takes those, like you and me, who could not bear to live here. Or like my father, who had no choice but to leave the human world."

"Then you do belong here. Some part of you."

I felt a brush of air like hoarfrost's fingers on my cheek. "Be careful," he said very softly. "She has held me fast since I was born. She will find a way to hold you, too, and another brier rose will bloom in the human world, that has its roots in this one."

"And beside it will grow a laurel, and a linden tree. Who is she? Does she have a name?"

He tried to answer. Leaves came out of his mouth instead of words. I cried out in terror, reaching out to him; my hands closed on shadow, on nothing. Leaves opened in his eyes and flowed like tears; leaves pushed through his heart. I tried to say his name; I had no voice, not even leaves. *Corbet,* my heart called over and over, until a brier tangled through the endless fall of ivy, and out of his heart a rose bloomed in answer.

She came to me then, cloaked in ivy instead of owl white. Her long fingers touched my wrist and circled it. Tears and words and blood all in the shape of leaves slid out of Corbet to twine into her hair. I could no longer see him, only the vague form of a man within the green: a finger, a pale gleam of hair, a blind eye among the leaves.

"You didn't come here for my name," she said, ignoring my broken, incoherent pleas. "You came for yours."

My mother walked through the grass and wildflowers toward us. Her dreaming eyes saw nothing, her skin was polished pearl. I took a step back; fingers as strong as tree root stopped me.

"She is still watching for him, Rois. Time pools here;

it has nowhere to go. A hundred years might pass in your world before I call her to me again, but if I call her in a hundred years, she will come. She'll tell us who came to her out of my wood, who gave you his eyes."

I could not move; I could not make a sound. And then I made a sound with my entire body, a silent scream that snapped through me and wrenched me free. The ivy around Corbet shook; I heard his sharp breath. Through the swirl of wind and light around me she spoke sweetly, but not to me.

"Let me help you. Who are you looking for?"

I saw my mother very clearly then, in one of those strange, timeless moments that seem to last forever between two words, or while a knife falls, just before it slips and cuts. She was scarcely older than Laurel when she died, I saw with horror. She had given me her hair and her light eyes, but not her mouth; that and her slender hands had gone to Laurel. She was pale as milk and so thin her skin had pared itself down to the bone. She did not seem to see her questioner; her eyes held too much light, too much memory. But she heard the question.

"He had no name," she answered. "He never spoke." Her dreaming voice was peaceful, remote. "I'll know him when he comes to me. I never see him clearly at first. He is a fall of light along the oak tree that stands behind the little well where the brier roses bloom. They open all summer long, and where their petals fall, that's where I lay my Rois to wait."

There was another question; I didn't hear. I shook like a naked child thrown into the dead of winter. I could not seem to cry; my tears had frozen in that cold.

"He came with summer. One such summer becomes every summer; it seems he came to me in all of them. I saw him and I lost myself. I followed the path of the sun to the wood, always, in my mind if I could not leave the house. It had nothing to do with the life I knew, any more than dreams do. And so I thought, when the dream was over, that I would wake."

I heard myself make a sound then; I put my hands over my mouth to stifle it. My mother did not hear. I did not exist, only the baby in her memories she had left beside the well.

"He never asked about Rois. He never spoke, any more than light speaks, until it changes, and then you understand and it is too late."

"Let her go," I whispered through my hands. "Let her go."

"She is searching for her heart. Humans think they lose such things here. She misplaced it in your world, left a hollow that nothing could fill until she wandered into light." She asked my mother, "Was he the first from the wood? Were there others?"

"No," my mother said. "No one else. No one ever except him."

I cried out then, moving toward my mother, trying to catch her eyes. "He is not here! You will never find him, ever, ever! He never loved you! Go back where you are loved!"

But it was like shouting in a dream, or under water. My mother, hearing no more questions, followed a breeze toward a distant pool of light. She faded into colors, into air, before she reached it.

I could not stand. I crouched on the ground, racked with cold, as if her ghost, her death, had passed through me. I could not cry, and I could not stop trembling. I felt a regard far colder than my mother's blindness, and looked up into sapphire eyes.

"I wonder whose child you are . . . I wonder if even she knew. But now you know where you belong. You have been coming to this place since you were born."

"My father is a farmer," I whispered numbly, without conviction. "I belong to his world."

"Then how did you see past his clods and endless furrows to come here?"

"The way my mother did. I followed someone. Like her, I could not help myself." I stood up, still shivering, wanting to go, not knowing where to go, because I didn't know anymore what love meant, or why we were not all better off without it.

I saw Corbet's eyes then, and his mouth, and one hand open among the leaves. His eyes held mine, more powerfully than any touch; they knew me. He whispered one word that was not a leaf, and I felt the deadly cold in me finally melt, my frozen tears break free.

"Rois."

"Yes," I told him. "I will come back."

Which is why, I supposed, she let me go.

Twenty-two

Stone walls closed around me. I stood at the hearth in Lynn Hall, in front of my pile of twigs and split kindling, that had only burned in some other world, and left me cold in this one. The silent rooms were smoky with late afternoon shadows. I had to go home, but somewhere beyond the pallid light, within the stones, Corbet had spoken my name, and I couldn't bear to leave the place where I was known. I knelt, folded myself against the cold, made myself small and still, something nameless in the winter, watching and being watched.

Don't leave me, he had said: a plea.

You must hold him, she had said: a promise.

She did not know me; I didn't know myself. I was something wild in her wood, as she was in mine, maybe human, maybe not, but even human I recognized her. My mother had called her, Laurel was calling her. She was the death of the heart, and she harvested in the dead of winter. She was transforming my world around me, reaching out to those I loved, changing them to suit her season. She had my mother, she had Corbet; she would take Laurel, she would take me, in the end, because I would follow my heart. But neither of us knew what I could or couldn't do within her wood.

I heard something whisper through the air, and turned. A white owl flew across the room into the tapestry. It gazed at me out of wide, golden eyes before it faded into formless thread. This time it didn't ask its mocking question. It only asked what it already knew.

She had said: You must be human to love.

Neither of us knew this Rois.

I got up finally, before the world turned black and my father came for me. Snow mingled with the fading light as I drove home; flakes, catching in my eyelashes, seemed too heavy to bear. The snow never seemed to touch the ground; everything blurred around me. I held the reins, but the horses chose their path, it seemed, carrying me beyond the daylight toward an unfamiliar dark.

But they stopped in a familiar place. My father, hearing the sleigh, came out to take the horses in. "Where have you been?" he kept asking. "Where have you been? In that cold house all this time?"

"Yes," I said. He looked at me closely, but blamed the raw winds for my reddened eyes. I did not know who to blame: him for not seeing enough, my mother for seeing too much in a fall of summer light. Neither, I decided; neither was to blame. Blame lay in another world; that much I could see clearly, even in the gathering night.

"You look terrible," my father said brusquely. "I was just beginning to think you were coming into some sense." He turned the horses toward the barn. "Between the two of you," I heard, and he added a few more things that only the horses heard.

I sat down to supper with him and Laurel, but I could barely eat. Something kept pushing into my throat when I tried to swallow. I would see my mother's pale face, her thin, thin fingers, and, haunted, I could not eat for her, so I did not want to eat. I felt Laurel watching me; she had achieved more convincingly than I the art of eating air.

"Rois," she said softly. The barest hint of expression troubled the dead calm in her face. "What did you find there?"

Ghosts, I thought. I hesitated; she would not believe nothing. Our father answered for me.

"Nothing," he said roundly, "and I don't want to hear any more of it, and that's the end of it."

But she had found something in my eyes more disturbing than nothing.

"Rois," she breathed, and I stood abruptly.

"Nothing," I repeated, and was as startled as they were by the fierceness in my voice. "You were right. So don't ask me again. And he is right. That's the end of it. So I wish you would eat something besides nothing."

I crawled into bed then without undressing, burrowed under wool and down. Laurel came up soon after;

she paused at the open door, a candle in her hand, guessing from my uneven breathing that I was still awake. She came in, and I pushed back out of the quilts.

"You know something," she said, her own eyes wide, luminous, holding mine. "You saw something in Lynn Hall that I missed. What was it?"

I had seen ghosts and memories, lovers made of air and leaves, nothing. I opened my mouth; nothing came out. She put her hand on my wrist. Her fingers were carved of wax; in the candlelight I could almost see bone. My throat closed in sudden fear; I forced words out. "I saw you," I whispered. "I saw you."

She was silent. Her hold slackened, her fingers slid away from me. "You're making no sense, Rois."

"You're doing exactly what our mother did. You're not eating, you're wasting away, waiting for someone to come to you out of the empty winter."

"She wasn't waiting for anyone. She loved our father."

"She went to the wood—she took me—"

Something flicked into her eyes: almost life, almost a memory. She blinked it away. "It's winter. You don't have enough to do, so you're imagining things. Telling stories to yourself. About our mother, about me, about Corbet." She laid a hand made of bird-bone, thistledown, on my shoulder. "Don't fret so much about me. This has nothing to do with our mother. I'm simply waiting for Corbet to come back."

I woke pushing windblown leaves away from my face, until leaves turned into a hillock of quilts under my hand, and the fierce winds blew out of my dream to rattle against the window. I looked out. A snow-ghost, trailing veils and clouds, engulfed my father on his way to the barn. He disappeared a moment, then reappeared, holding onto his rope. I dressed, ate breakfast alone. Laurel drifted down later, her step so frail I barely heard the stairs creak. She took her place beside the fire, wrapped in a quilt, her hair hanging lankly down her back. I brought her tea and buttered bread. She thanked me, but her eyes didn't move from the wild, snow-streaked winds calling her beyond the window.

Perrin knocked on the door later, startling me. Laurel must have seen him coming; her expression never changed. Or else, I thought in sudden horror, she would have greeted Corbet himself with the same indifference: She waited now for something else entirely.

Perrin gave me a pot of soup that his mother had made for Laurel. I took it to Beda, who set it over the fire and sent me back with a cup of brandy for Perrin.

He looked, making conversation for two, as if he needed it.

"How could you find your way through this?" I asked him.

He cast a grim glance at me, then realized I meant the weather. "It's not snowing, just windy. If snow starts coming down, I might have to live here a while, with the wind this bad." He looked at Laurel, who was a pale profile within her limp hair. He touched an embroidered violet on her quilt lightly. "Will you eat a little of my mother's soup? She'll want to know. She'll feel badly if you don't. She made it for you."

Laurel dragged her eyes from the window, gazed at him across snowbound fields. "That was nice of her," she said politely. "Please tell her it was good."

They were both silent when I returned with the soup. I handed Laurel a bowl; she took half a spoonful, said something perfunctory, then sat holding it awkwardly, letting it grow cold. Her eyes went to the window. I heard Perrin take an unsteady breath. But he kept his voice steady, speaking to me when Laurel didn't answer. When words finally failed us both, he remembered the flute on the shelf behind Laurel.

He picked it up and began to play softly. Laurel's face turned quickly from the window at the first sweet notes. She stared at Perrin as if she had not known he was there. Then she felt the bowl in her hands. She set it down, and leaned back, pulling the quilt closely around her. Firelight brushed across her face, melting its stiffness, as she watched Perrin; a forgotten expression surfaced. I left them there, to sit on the stairs and listen, and remember how we all once were such an endless time ago, when Laurel loved Perrin and I loved no one, and only the season would change.

Perrin spoke to Laurel and played, and spoke again; I heard her murmur once or twice. He left her finally, came to the door looking pale and tired. He said softly, tying his cloak, "She listened, but she barely spoke and she didn't eat at all. When I stopped playing, she'd hear the wind, and her attention would drift again. It's as if she's under a spell."

"Yes," I said hollowly. "Will you come back soon?"

"Tomorrow. Even if I have to walk blind through a blizzard. I'll go to the village first, see if Blane can come up with anything to help her."

"Thank you."

"Not so long ago I wished Corbet Lynn off the face of the earth. Now I'd give my heart to see him back, because that's what it would cost me. But I'd give it, for her sake."

He kissed my cheek, and went down our father's path to the barn.

The next morning, Laurel did not get out of bed. She apologized to our father when he came up to her. He clamped his teeth around his unlit pipe, glimpsing another nightmare; I saw the terror in his eyes.

"I'll be all right," Laurel said to him. She seemed genuinely sorry to trouble him by doing something that only I did in the winter. "I just need to rest a little. I just feel tired. I don't know why."

She didn't sleep, though. When I brought her tea, or soup, or one of Beda's ginger cakes, I found her awake watching the snow, her face calm, remote, as colorless as snow. I wished desperately that she would pace, or weep, or curse Corbet for leaving her, and consign him to the death's-head smile and pitiless embrace of winter. I wanted to throw her teacup across the room, shout at her for being so blind to herself, so selfish and cruel not to choose to live for our sakes, if she could find no other reason. But she would only tell me that it was winter and I was imagining things again; she was fine; she was just not hungry now.

I sat with her in the late afternoon, brushing her hair,

which was longer, unpinned, than I remembered. It looked thin now; it had lost its polished darkness. The winds died finally, leaving an eerie stillness over the world. I saw Perrin in his sleigh, a long way down the road, looking, with his furs and painted runners, at once courageous and powerless as he moved between the vast white planes of earth and sky. He had brought Blane with him.

The apothecary came face to face with the same nightmare, though he hid it better. He pulled up a chair beside the bed, listening expressionlessly as Laurel apologized for bringing him out for no reason in such bad weather. He sent our father and Perrin downstairs while he examined her; then he sent me down while he questioned her.

I found my father chewing memories and his unlit pipe beside the fire. Perrin sat with the flute in his hands, turning it slowly, watching firelight streak silver along it and vanish. "Play," I begged. He tried; a few sweet notes whistled into air and he lowered it again, wordlessly, to watch the light.

Blane came down finally. His eyes went first to my father and then to Perrin. "Corbet Lynn," he said. It was a question.

My father made an effort, then waved the entire question at Perrin and reached for a taper.

"He caught her off-balance," Perrin answered wearily. "He caught us all."

"And then he vanished." Blane rubbed his eyes. "Or he died. Unfortunately, he's the only cure I can find for Laurel."

"That's all?" my father asked incredulously. "Corbet Lynn?"

The apothecary looked at him silently a moment. "It's more," he said carefully, "than we had before." He moved to the fire, stared at it, his spare face bloodless, haunted. He added reluctantly, "I don't know if it's even Corbet she wants now."

"Well, then, what—" My father stumbled a step toward him, his own face tallow; Blane held his eyes wordlessly.

Perrin's hands clenched. He said abruptly, "He's all she wants and if he's what she wants, then I'll find him if I have to shovel out the wood. Somebody must remember where he came from. There must be a letter from someone around the place. Other people have such things in their lives, even Corbet must, though it seems he might as well have lived in another world for all the ties he has to this one. There must be something."

"Yes." Blane turned to get his cloak. "I gave her nightshade," he added to me, "to help her sleep. I'll come again tomorrow." Perrin, his mouth tight, rose to take him home. The apothecary dropped a hand on his shoulder. "The most important thing is for her to begin to eat again. Once she takes another look at life, she might start thinking the better of what she thinks she wants out of it."

Perrin took him back to the village. I sat with my father while he smoked, and watched the fire, and I watched the firelight and shadows flow across his face like expressions I could not read. I knew that in strangely different ways he had reached the same thoughts about my mother. *Had she?* the shifting shadows asked. *Was that what she? Why she?* He did not go farther; I went alone into that dark question. *Are you*? I asked him silently, searching intently for some hint of myself in his face. Or am I winter's inhuman child?

He felt my eyes and met them finally; for a moment we questioned each other wordlessly. Then his hard face melted under a caress of light and he shifted, shaking his head. He could see no one in those distant, empty fields that had held my mother spellbound. No one she could possibly have cried out to, longed for, until longing pared her down to bone, and then to earth, and only her longing was left to haunt us all.

"It's eerie, though," he breathed, as if all this time we had been talking. "It's as if Laurel inherited some weakness from her mother. And since she knows no other name for it—" He broke off, rising restlessly, leaving the name for it troubling the air between us. "Do you remember how you and Laurel used to ask about his past? What was it he said? Where he had come from?"

"He never said."

"He must have said something, some hint. I'll go to the village tomorrow with Perrin, help him ask . . ."

I left my father drinking apple brandy beside the fire, and went upstairs to Laurel's room. She slept without moving, so quietly I had to stand over her to hear her breathe. She made so little noise now; she used so little air. She willed herself smaller, smaller; soon she would take nothing from life, neither air nor space nor time, and life would have no claim on her. I felt a wild grief rise in me at the thought that my eyes would look for her, since I had looked at her every day of my life, and she would leave me nothing to see. I would not know that new world in which she did not exist. I heard the winds in the dark, and I knew they called her; if I looked out the window, I would see ghosts of shimmering snow drifting around the house, peering in every window, whispering her name. The dead of winter.

I went downstairs, made myself a tea to keep me awake so that I could guard her against the dead. I sat beside her in the dark, ignoring the thin fingers shaking the window, the impatient shrieks, the luring calls. As long as I could hear her breathe, we were all safe. In spite of the tea, my eyes grew heavy. Once I thought she opened eyes like cold sapphire stars to look at me, and I started awake, spilling tea. I put the cup down finally, and knelt on the floor, resting my head in my arms beside her pillow, where I could hear her even in my dreams.

I stood in the wood. Now it was a grim and shadowy tangle of thick dark trees, dead vines, leafless branches that extended twigs like fingers to point toward the heartbeat of hooves. The buttermilk mare, eerily pale in that silent wood, galloped through the trees; tree boles turned toward it like faces. A woman in her wedding gown rode with a man in black; he held the reins with one hand and his smiling bride with the other. She wore lace from throat to heel; the roses in her chestnut hair glowed too bright a scarlet, mocking her bridal white. Black swirled around the bridegroom as he slowed the horse; the hood of his cloak slid back to reveal his golden hair, his cold, cold eyes. When they stopped, her expression began to change from a pleased, astonished smile, to confusion and growing terror. *What twilight wood is this?* she asked him. *What dead, forgotten place?*

It is our home, he answered. He held her tightly as she began to struggle. She screamed, and he laughed, and so did all the gnarled, twisted faces watching within the trees.

"Rois." I lifted my head, hearing Laurel's voice. We are in the same dream, I thought, terrified. It is no dream. "Rois." Her fingers found my wrist and gripped it with more strength than I thought she had, to take me with her into that dreadful wood, or to cling to life so she would not have to go alone. Then she turned away from me. I felt the hard floor under my knees, heard her breathing again, so faint it would barely disturb cobweb.

Wind rattled at the door; I got up, shivering, as cold within as if I had died. I went downstairs quietly, so quietly that my father, still awake, staring into the fire, did not stir. I opened the door, watched the swirling blackness slowly shape itself into a restless hoof, a starry eye, silvery harness, the snow-trimmed edge of a hooded mantle. I could not see the rider's face; I did not know who watched me: she with winter's icy fires, or he with the bridegroom's cold, familiar eyes.

I said to both of them, "Let her stay. I will go with you."

The rider bent, held out a hand. I closed the door, and rode the dark winds into midnight.

Twenty-three

She took me to Lynn Hall.

I saw her face as we entered; winds slammed the door open ahead of us, pulled at her cloak, her hood, until it slid back. With odd relief I saw her eyes, less terrible than his, because she was nothing I had ever loved. Lynn Hall had changed again. This time she showed me how her secret wood devoured it, in a monstrous tangle of root and vine that wove into its stones and massed across its gaping roof. Past and future and the timeless wood scattered broken pieces of themselves within two rooms. Nial Lynn's marble floor lay broken and weathered by the years, even while his blood or Tearle's flowed darkly across it. A curve of tree root so thick it must have circled the world had pushed through the floor beneath Corbet's table, on which someone's stale beer stood growing staler in a cup. The tapestry flickered in and out of existence, now solid, swarming with white, gold-eyed owls; now transparent, glinting threads of light. The bed was a heap of brambles on which pillows lay neatly encased in lace. Here and there among the brambles wild roses bloomed and withered, bloomed elsewhere.

Ivy grew up the wall beside the hearth, gripping the stones, flowing along the ceiling, as if its leaves were fingers feeling for escape. I stared at it, searching for Corbet in the green, since he was nowhere else in the hall. She spoke his name. Ivy trembled and breathed, sighed a human sigh. On the mantel, misshapen candles of wood and wax flamed suddenly. Light touched him into shape; leaves became his eyes; leaves turned into words.

He looked dazed, waking out of his green dream, as if he couldn't remember why he had a human shape. Then he saw me and remembered how to speak.

"Rois."

"Rois has come to stay with us."

He looked from me to her silently, and waited. Her cloak had fallen; she wore, I saw with horror, the dress that Laurel had worn in my dream, only torn, faded, and stained with blood, as if it had been used long ago at some disastrous wedding. I said quickly, "I will do whatever you want, if you promise me that Laurel will be safe."

"You will do what I want. And then perhaps I'll tell you about Laurel."

I could not run away from her this time; she would reach Laurel faster than I could. She smiled, her face the color of bone, her hair as white as cobweb now, something very old and very beautiful, nameless in the human world, and as dangerous as anything we could not name.

I said what I had to. "I will do what you want."

"No," Corbet breathed. "Rois, no— " She glanced at him; he swallowed, then spat out a word in green.

"Rois chose to come here," she answered. "To be with you in place of Laurel. She would have found her way back to you and to this place with or without me; this is her birthright. I will give you what you dreamed of, Rois. You will marry Corbet in Lynn Hall." I stared at her. Leaves came out of Corbet, the same word endlessly repeated. She only said to him, "You can fill this hall with leaves until you no longer see her, but you will wed her here and now. Living in your father's house, raising children for me, you won't be tempted to leave me again."

My name bloomed, blood-red, out of his mouth. I put my hands over mine. "Please—let him speak—"

"Not until that no becomes yes." She waited; he shook his head mutely, swallowing leaves.

"Please," I begged her again. His eyes, holding mine, were narrowed as against the fiercest of winds; his face held no more color than the stone behind him. "Maybe—maybe he doesn't love me."

"Maybe he doesn't, but he will never leave you. The rose will wed the ivy in Lynn Hall, and they will be so tightly bound that to uproot one will be to uproot the other, and both will live or die together."

He stopped struggling to find words then; his face grew very still. I saw the word in his eyes before he spoke. My own eyes burned with bitter tears. A shadow-marriage in a shadowland was all we would ever have; we had left truth behind us in another time. His head bowed; he did not look at either of us.

"Yes."

She smiled her feral smile that held no trace of love or laughter. "Then light the tapers and prepare the hall. I will bring the wedding guests."

It took me a moment to realize that she was no longer with us. Corbet gazed without moving at the air where she had vanished; his eyes held a bleak despair as he contemplated our future. Then he looked at me.

I saw the ghost of his grandfather, in his pale, cold face, his mouth set in a thin, bloodless line. I do not know you, I thought suddenly, as fear rilled through me. I do not know you at all in this place.

He saw my fear; he only turned away to light a line of tapers pinned on thorns along the wall. "You tried," he said to the wall.

"I didn't know—I had to, for Laurel—"

"I know."

"And I don't even know—" My hands closed tightly. "She won't even tell me if Laurel—"

"She never gives, she never yields." He still faced the wall, but without moving, staring at the thorns. The taper was burning close to his fingers. He did not feel it, or maybe he did not care. He added softly, "I asked you for the impossible. I should never have done that. But I had no one else to turn to. And you were with me at every turn. I'm sorry."

I whispered, "And every turn led us here. Back into these two small rooms."

He felt the taper fire then; he shook it away from him into the grate. He said helplessly, "I tried—"

"I know." I shivered, bone-cold. "You warned me."

I moved to the hearth, where a log lay half-burned, eaten open to its heart, fuming sullenly. I knelt beside it. Corbet lit another taper and touched more candles caught on thorns, in the crook of roots, until it seemed that within the wild roil of root and stone fiery roses bloomed everywhere around us.

Our eyes met. I heard the winter close around us, the shrieking, fighting winds racing toward us across a barren wasteland. His hand moved toward me, dropped helplessly, holding air and firelight. I did not try to touch him.

And then I saw the shadows move around us, as if they had been silently listening, waiting for the moment when there was nothing left for us to say. Candlelight brushed an ivory curve of cheek, froze in a jewel, burned in an unblinking eye. I could see no one very clearly except her, moving slowly toward us, gathering a bouquet of burning roses from among the thorns.

"You must have flowers." She placed them in my hands. The flames grew still, shaped petals of cold fire. "And a veil." She pulled the tapestry loose; it slid lightly down, silver and gold overflowing her hands. She drew it over my hair, my shoulders; it felt at once airy and clinging, like feathers. "And a ring." She opened her hand and I saw the golden circle through which I had once watched the sky.

I looked at her blindly, remembering it falling in the daylight, in the autumn night, from my mother's hand, from her hand.

"I gave this to you once before," she said, and I listened for the faint, mocking laughter around her. But no one laughed. The smile in her eyes might only have been the light from Corbet's taper. "This time Corbet must give it to you." She took the taper from him. "Rois to wood, rose to ivy, maid to mortal man you will wed, in time and beyond time, and forever in my wood."

She dropped the ring into Corbet's hand.

I lifted my hand to take the ring, and felt the unexpected warmth of timebound flesh and bone that mortals needed to continue their brief, drab, passionate lives.

My fingers locked around his wrist.

I felt him start. A word broke through the endless winter in his eyes. But she gave him no time to say it, except in leaves. Green wove through the air where he had been, and I felt tears burn in my throat because she had hidden him from me again. But I held him, vine and leaf and unspoken word, while gold slid through leaves to break the silence against the marble floor.

"Yes," I said, to the wood and all his ghosts.

I heard the sudden, fierce cry of wind blasting through the door. All the candles spun crazily on their sconces and fell, burning out like stars. I could only see her face in the firelight, and her wild, hoarfrost hair streaming like snow on the wind. Around us, her following, her ghosts, shifted uncertainly and whispered. Some laughed; again I heard the tiny, silvery bells, their singing brief and oddly jangled.

I tightened my hold on the ivy, racked by wind that should have torn the leaves from the vine and the vine from my fingers. Not even that wind was strong enough. I couldn't speak, under the fuming, blue-black fire in her eyes. But I held her words fast, as fast as I held our lives. She had spoken, she had said; her own words challenged her.

She minced no words now. "Laurel will die for this."

I swallowed, forced out words as dry as leaves. "Not if I bring Corbet back with me. She'll see him and remember how to live."

"You will die here for nothing and I will keep your ghost. You will not free Corbet and you will never leave."

"I will." My voice shook badly; again I heard the faint, tuneless laughter. "You told me how."

"I played with you. You were a foolish rabbit caught between worlds in my rose vines, blinded by moonlight and thinking you wanted the moon. You had no idea what you asked for."

"No, I didn't then." I shifted closer to the ivy; it clung to stone and thorn against her fury. "But you told me how to take it."

"And you saw me to ask. You don't have human eyes, a human heart. You can't live in the human world—why do you think you pulled time and dreams apart to find my wood?"

"He kept crying out from your wood for help. You killed his father. You turn his words to leaves. You take away his eyes, his voice. You don't love him. Why do you care where he goes?"

"Because he is mine, of my blood and of the wood.

Love and hate are nothing more than leaves here; he knows that. He was not born to learn them."

"He does know them! He is human, except for the sliver of ice in his heart that came from you. It won't melt here, and it will destroy us both. Let him go. You only want him to reflect you, to see your power and beauty when you look at him. Nothing more than that. It was his human heart that led him to my world—you had no use for it here."

"He has no heart." Her eyes burned still darker, holding mine. "I took it from him the moment he was born. And I will take yours."

I felt a thin arm sliding through my fingers. I caught my breath in horror, tightening my grip before I lost it. Then I nearly lost it again when I looked for Corbet's face and found my mother.

"Rois," she said reproachfully. "What are you doing?"

I couldn't find my voice. "You are ivy," I whispered. "You are Corbet. You are not—"

"You belong here," she said. "With me. And with your father." Her face, so like mine, transfixed me. *I am you,* it seemed to say. *I am your fate.*

"I have a father."

"Your true father is of this wood. You know that. You always knew. You saw her wood in every shift of light, in every secret shadow. You searched for it until you found it. You recognized it because you have his eyes."

"I don't want a father I have never seen! I don't care who he was! And how can I have a father here? You loved one summer and died in winter and I was already born. Here love doesn't last beyond a season—it can't survive her winter."

"There were other summers before I died. Others from the wood."

"You are lying to me! You aren't even my mother—you're leaves, even your words are leaves."

"I am your mother, Rois. You can see me here. You can speak to me. Stay with me. You love Corbet and you love the wood. Stay here with us. You could never have found your way here unless you belong here."

"You did," I said through tears. "And look what happened to you. You can't love me here." I spoke to them both: to her and Corbet, clinging to them both. "You can't love me here."

"Don't leave me," she pleaded. "Don't leave me, Rois. Don't."

"Come with me," I begged, gripping her so tightly that if she had not been illusion, and a ghost besides, I would have left an imprint on her bones. "Corbet."

Her face changed. His face and not his face gazed back at me, and I felt an animal's fear prickle through me, such as Corbet's father must have felt under those powerful, barren grey eyes.

"So you are playing a little game now, Rois," he said. The sudden twist of his arm in my lax hold nearly freed him; I caught him with both hands then, held on grimly, mindlessly, evading his eyes. I felt something shock through us both; sudden pain threw me to my knees.

"You're dead," I whispered breathlessly, tasting blood. "Your son killed you. Nial Lynn."

"Nothing dies in the wood," he said. "You saw that. Here no one can harm me. But I will hurt you if you do not let go of me. Love cowers from pain. Love hides itself. Love whimpers like a dog and runs."

I whimpered like a dog. Roses bloomed in my hands; their thorns clung to me as tightly as I clung to them. Blood streaked my fingers, as if the blood-red petals bled. And then they flamed.

I could not see anything but fire. Sweat and tears ran down my face. Love hurts, I thought crazily. Love hurts.

"But I knew that," I said through blood and tears, still kneeling, hunched with pain, clinging to my burning bridal flowers. "You didn't have to tell me that."

"I am doing this for your own good," Nial Lynn said. It sounded true: Not a tremor of pleasure disturbed the dead calm in his voice. "You have grown too wild, Rois. You must calm your imaginings. Even now you imagine you are here, trying to rescue someone you think you love, who in the waking world scarcely noticed you. He did not love you there, so you dream a world where he must need you, where he must be grateful to you. That is why you are forcing yourself to suffer this in your dreams. So that he will be grateful and love you. In your dreams."

My skin was melting from my bones; finger bones were melting as I held his burning hands. I sobbed without noise; everything burned, even words. "Then I must end the dream to end the pain. And it will never end, ever, ever, for either of us, if I let you go. I must hold you fast, because you are part of him. You will trap him here and turn his heart to ice if I let go of you. In my dreams."

The fire flared in my face. I jerked back, crying, feeling my face begin to melt. I heard his voice beyond the flames.

"All you must do is stop the dream. Stop dreaming. Rois. Wake. Go back to the human world. Forget this world, because this moment is the only one you will ever remember of it when you try to remember." I could not see; I felt my eyes begin to burn. I screamed again, without sound, and drew in fire like air. My bones began to burn, and then my heart.

"Rois. Wake. Rois."

I heard myself say, somehow, for I had no lips, no throat, to speak with, "I must hold this dream fast, no matter what shape it takes, for it is only a dream; there is no fire, and no pain, and no Nial Lynn. You are dead. You have no power anymore. You are dead. Your son killed you and I know why, and when I pass your grave I will spit on it. I will cut down any flowers growing on it. I will—"

I felt hands in my hands, cool strong fingers in mine. I had hands again. I had a mouth, eyes. I closed my eyes, held the hands to my face, and kissed petals of blood across them.

"Rois."

I looked up. My hands tightened; it did not hurt any longer to hold. But I was not sure what I held.

He said very wearily, "Rois, you must let me go." I saw his grandfather again in his cold eyes; I saw the fey beauty he had inherited from her, that lured me so powerfully, and then loosed me and turned away, leaving me with nothing but my hopeless, desperate longings. "I thought I could not lie to you, but I was wrong. I have been lying all along. I have never loved you. I don't want you here with me. If I loved anyone—if I can love anyone at all—it was Laurel. You know that. You have always known that." I stared up at him, wordless. He knelt suddenly in front of me, holding my eyes, letting me see his face clearly. "I can't let you go through this torment for nothing. I will make you miserable if you stay here. You have already sensed that. I can see it in your eyes. You are afraid of me in this world. You are right to be afraid."

I whispered his name.

"There's something in you difficult to love. Something scarcely human. You are too wild, Rois; you aren't like other women. It would be barely possible to love you in the human world, impossible to love you here. How could you imagine that I would really forget Laurel?" He glanced at my fingers, frozen around his. "It's better for both of us. I'll go to Laurel, she'll recover, and you'll be much happier without me. You'll lose nothing."

I swallowed nothing, dust, hot ashes. My heart hammered sickly. Still his gaze trapped mine; I could not look away. He had found all my secret fears and loosed them one by one; they swarmed through me, howling, showing a bloody tooth. "I can't leave." My lips felt icy, as if I had been kissed by winter. "I want to stay with you. Perhaps you will love me in time."

"Rois, I have tried—you've seen that—"

I felt sorrow slide, cold and silent, down my face. "You're lying. You're not Corbet—"

"You know me, Rois. Your heart knows me. Just as you know that what I say is true. I am sorry. What Laurel and I feel for each other is far different from anything you can imagine. You have tried to help me, and I am grateful. But love is not gratitude. I can't be content with you because of that."

"No." The word hurt like a stone in my throat. "You can't." His face blurred in my eyes; I blinked it clear again. Nothing else seemed clear to me; everything he said to me I had said to myself. "But, Corbet, there were things—between us—"

"You imagined many of them. You wanted them to be true, and so they were. But only to you." He dropped his head, kissed my icy fingers. "Now you must leave me. Go back to Laurel. She needs you far more than I. I'll come to her soon. One day you will forgive me."

I could not argue with him; I did not know anymore what I was doing or why. I clung to all I knew: his hands, her words. "She said I must hold fast to you—"

He sighed. "Rois. You're only holding fast to some dream of love—nothing real."

"No matter what shape you take—"

"Rois."

"No matter what face you show—"

"Stop trying to help me. I don't want your help. I don't need you."

"Don't leave me here. Don't leave me. Don't. You said that to me. And then you said my name."

"You were dreaming—"

"I will give you what you want." I could not find my voice, only a husk of one; it could barely pass through the fire in my throat. I clung more tightly to his hands, and held his eyes; I saw the first touch of icy anger struggle with his patience. "I will leave you. I won't trouble you any longer with my love. But I want to give you something first. With my love."

"What?" he asked indifferently.

"Freedom. From me, from this house, from her wood. I will hold you fast until you stand free of us all. And then I will leave you."

I heard him say my name, just before the winds tore at him again. I lost hold of one hand; I held the other in both of mine as the wind tried to carry him away. I felt ivy again, and then a human wrist, and again ivy, and then the ivy closed around my wrist.

Winds screamed through the sudden dark. "Who gave you your eyes?"

I knew then. I had been looking at the answer all my life, at all its beauty, its seasons, its ever-changing faces of life and death.

"The wood."

The ivy held fast to me then, as fast as I held it. Vine turned to bone, leaf to word.

"Rois," he said, and I felt a rose bloom on my lips. I held him through the winter dark, through all my dreams until I woke.

Twenty-four

I lay awake a long time before I opened my eyes. I heard soft movements through the house, a word or two. I smelled bread baking, and a handful of dried flower petals simmering sweetly above the fire. Perhaps that had wakened me: the scent of spring.

But it was still winter, I found, when I finally opened my eyes. Snow crusted the barn roof; the sky was stone-grey, the distant wood still leafless. No smoke rose from Lynn Hall.

I gazed, perplexed, across the snowbound fields. My hands still felt the ivy the wind had tried to wrench from me; my bones remembered fire peeling them like twigs. I heard Nial's voice: This is the only thing you will remember . . . You imagine you are here. Stop the dream.

I remembered Laurel.

I pushed myself up at the thought. The floor felt icy

as my bare feet hit it. Winter still wailed around the house, slid long, thin fingers through chinks and crevices. What had I done? I wondered, pushing hair out of my eyes. What had I done right or wrong? A gold ring, burning roses, my mother's face, Corbet's despairing eyes—my dream scattered piecemeal through my head. I had gone into the heart of winter, pulled Corbet out of it into this world, so that he could ride to our door on his buttermilk mare and find Laurel and say her name, so that she would remember who she was, what life was, before she left it.

Maybe, I thought desperately as I swung the door open, that's where he was now: riding to our door.

I went down the hall to Laurel's room, feeling a yoke of fear prick painfully at my neck, across my shoulders. I tried to enter noiselessly, but her door-latch slipped in my fingers, rattled. She stirred slightly and I breathed again, clinging to the door a moment, watching her.

She looked like a woman made of silk and straw, so fragile that the wind outside could have blown her apart in a breath. Her skin molded itself against her bones. Her eyelids, frail as paper, lifted, as if she felt my eyes. She gazed at me senselessly a moment before she said my name.

I went to her, knelt beside the bed. The blue veins in her wrists were so clear beneath the skin, I could almost see them pulse. She lifted a finger, gave me a feathery touch.

"I had the strangest dream," she said.

"What?"

"I'm not sure . . ." She was silent, her eyes fixed on

some memory. She drew a faint breath. "I think you were in it. I don't know. All I see now are colors. I hear a voice, but I don't understand the words. You know the way it is when you try to remember dreams. Even what you do remember makes no sense. . . ."

"Sometimes it does."

"I mean, in the waking world."

I let it go; suddenly I understood very little. "Would you like me to bring you some tea?"

"No." Her eyes went to the window. I felt my own eyes widen and burn. I had done nothing; I had dreamed, and even in my dream I had done nothing. Or worse, none of it had been a dream, and I had done nothing right.

I felt her hand again on my arm. "This endless winter . . . Rois. Do you know what I would like? Some hot milk." I nodded and got up, not looking at her so that she would not see my tears. Her voice stopped me at the door. "I smell bread baking. Rois, could you bring me some warm bread, too, when it's out?" I turned to stare at her. She was not looking out the window now; she was thinking of food.

"What else?" My voice caught on something too big to swallow. "Butter? An egg?"

"Butter, yes. That's all. I think. Thank you."

I went out. I was halfway downstairs, when I had to sit, trembling, holding my bones together, blinking so that I could see more clearly what appeared to be true: Laurel wanted to eat.

"Rois," my father breathed at the bottom of the

stairs. I looked down, saw the terror in his eyes, and then saw myself, barefoot, in my nightgown, crouched and shaking on the stairs.

"It's all right," I said. I did not recognize my voice. "She just wants breakfast."

"She wants—"

"She's hungry."

He gripped the railing. I saw his face before he turned to sit down on the bottom step. He could not speak too clearly, either. "What—what does she want?"

"Hot milk. Hot bread and butter."

"Oh." It came out like the sound he might have made the first time he saw Laurel. I saw him shake. I stumbled down to him, my father in this world, in every world, and held him tightly. There Beda found us both, and left us both, her own eyes red, to get the apple brandy.

My father intercepted Salish on his sleigh, and sent a message to Perrin and to the apothecary. Perrin arrived first, with more soup from his mother; we hovered around Laurel, counting every mouthful. Later, the apothecary checked her, noted the faint flush of life beneath her skin, the sudden interest in her eyes.

"What did you give her?" he asked me incredulously.

I could not tell him. I still saw how closely her skin clung to the lovely line of bone in her face, how her eyes held distances beyond the defined horizons of our small world. She had gone as far as we could go from one another and still come back. She knew it, I could tell; she kept me beside her, watching me sew or sip tea; she wanted me with her even while she napped. It was as if she needed to tell me something but did not know how, or maybe even what; she wanted me with her because I already knew.

She finally found the strength, one afternoon, to go downstairs and sit beside the fire. She watched the fire, while I set a crooked patch in our father's trousers. Wind scattered snow like chaff; it was hard to tell whether the whirling flakes fell from the roof or from the sky. Laurel's eyes were drawn to the window; I watched her, poking myself now and then, as I sewed. She had come back without Corbet; so had I, and neither of us had spoken his name.

She said softly, "It seems so like a dream. As if someone had cast a spell over me. I don't understand what I was thinking." She looked at me. "It seems so impossible now, to think of any man that way."

I nodded, frowning hard over my patch. I could not find Corbet anywhere in my dreams; I had no idea what world I had left him in. Perhaps I had only imagined a world and him in it; I could not make that last, impossible, magical gesture, and pull him from my head into the real world. It seemed, considering how completely he had vanished, most likely. But still I had to frown tears away, of worry and loss and simple exasperation, because I did not know who I had rescued from the wood: Laurel, or Corbet, or all of us, or if, in the end, I had only rescued myself.

Laurel's eyes strayed back to the window. "But I do wonder what happened to him. Did anyone ever hear?"

"No."

"He was so alone in that place . . . No wonder he

turned to us. I think that's why he left: He really could not live in that old ruin with all its memories. He left to find some other life than Nial Lynn's."

I looked at her, astonished at her calm. "You're not angry at him for leaving you?"

"I don't think about him," she said softly. "Where I went, I went alone, and that's what I think about, what I have to understand. Sometimes I wonder if what I did had as much to do with our mother as with Corbet. I watched her die. Maybe, when Corbet left me so suddenly, it was like another death. I grieved in some strange way for both of them."

I wanted to ask then, but I didn't know how to circle around the question and hope she would answer without noticing. Finally, I just asked. "You watched for Corbet," I said, staring at an uneven stitch. "You made me wonder who our mother might have watched for. Who vanished out of her life and never returned."

"Yes," she said, astonishing me again. "The thought has crossed my mind, these past few days. Who she might have felt such passion for, to abandon her own life when he abandoned her."

"Who?" I breathed. "Do you know?"

But she only shook her head. "If there was anyone, she couldn't have loved him very long. The whole village would have guessed at anything longer than half a season. Longer than a week, more likely. And then our father would have known."

"He never—"

"No. You see how he is about her. There's not a shadow of mistrust in all his memories." She looked at me then, her eyes the smoky-grey of the fading light over the fields, no longer haunted, still unfamiliar in their calm. "You brought this up before. You said I was doing what she did."

"Well, I wondered."

She held my eyes a moment longer, glimpsing something—a cascade of brier roses, maybe, a fall of light. Perhaps she had been there, as a child, perhaps she had seen . . .

Perhaps there had never been anything at all to see.

I saw snowdrops in the snow one morning, and the yellow buds of crocuses. It did not seem possible that this harsh winter could ever end, but the crocus did not lie. Snow fluttered in the air, but melted as it touched the ground. As days passed, patches of brown earth began to appear in the fields. I watched the last of winter rattle in an icy sheet off the barn roof, break into pieces on the ground. One day it rained. Laurel, whom I had helped wash and feed and dress without even thinking about it, finally pushed me away that morning, laughing. She was still thin, but she moved easily now, and her skin had lost the fragile, waxen pallor she had gotten from wandering among ghosts. We sat outside that afternoon for the first time, watching sunlight slip between the swollen clouds to ignite a sudden glitter of raindrops all around us, on branch and harrow tooth and stone. I could not see enough, I thought; I could not smell enough of earth, and rain, and the scent of rain on the slowly budding branches. I needed more eyes, another nose. So I complained to Laurel, and she laughed again, which seemed as improbable a sound as the sound of returning birds.

Then she put her arm around me tightly, kissed my cheek. "Thank you," she whispered, "for not leaving me alone this winter. For staying with me."

I was silent, surprised: I must have become more human in spite of myself. My thoughts veered abruptly; I tugged them back into here and now, afraid of the secret and dangerous wood within, afraid to wonder what was dream and what was truth, and how much of either of those was love.

Perrin rode into the yard then, splashing mud and water. He dismounted beside the porch and handed me some early violets. I dropped my face into them and breathed, feeling their sweet scent flow into my blood. Laurel and Perrin studied each other, searching for signs of new life. I saw some in the calm in Perrin's eyes, the faint, wry crook of his mouth. Sunlight had flushed the color into Laurel's skin, or maybe Perrin had. He smiled a little.

"You look beautiful," he said to her. He sat down on the steps, cast a practiced glance at our father's furrows. Laurel picked up the piece of linen she was embroidering with sunflowers for Beda. Perrin's eyes had snagged on distances; suddenly we were all looking where he looked, beyond the fields to the patch of wood that hid Lynn Hall.

"Whatever happened to him?" Perrin breathed. "What happened? I've been waiting for them to find his body thawing along the road somewhere, but he vanished like a ghost." His face turned swiftly then to Laurel. "I'm sorry."

She shook her head, her eyes still on the cloud and

blazing blue where the chimney smoke would have drifted. "It's all right. I wonder, too, still." She drew her needle through the linen, painted a petal with yellow thread, while Perrin watched her. She seemed to hear his thoughts; she said slowly, "I wonder, but I don't look for him. When I think back that far, to what happened between us, I don't recognize myself. Now I hardly remember what did happen. If anything did at all, it happened to someone else." She met his eyes. "That's how it seems."

He nodded, not smiling now. "Do you miss him?"

"No," she said softly. "No more than I miss what I was when I did miss him."

For a while Perrin appeared sporadically, like the sun, not saying much, not staying long. And then the leaves began to open on the trees and he came every day, riding into the yard while I watched the sun flame behind the wood, then slowly fade. Spring brought back familiar human sounds as well as birds. Our father whistled, going from barn to house; I heard him and Perrin laugh together, muddy from plowing, too redolent with fertilizer to come into the house.

One night, going upstairs after supper, I heard Perrin play the flute again.

It brought tears to my eyes, memories I did not want to acknowledge. It also made me suddenly restless, impatient to feel wet grass under my feet, taste the wild strawberries. I wanted to drink the cold sweet water from the well, and see the new leaves covering the rose vines. I sat on the steps and listened, and thought of the wood at night, and how the moonlight would catch in the wet, silvery curves of branches, hang trembling from a leaf.

The playing stopped. I heard Laurel's gentle voice, teasing a little, our father's chuckle, Perrin's unruffled answer. I went up quietly, feeling the new leaves opening in me, catching light.

The next morning, I rode into the village with my father's winter boots to have the leaks cobbled out of them, and to get some salve for the cows from the apothecary. I told him about Laurel as he put the salve into a jar. As usual, his impassive face said very little; his eyes told me much.

"I thought she would die," he said simply. "That terrible winter night. I could not see any hope for her."

"None of us could, then."

"She never heard from Corbet?" I shook my head. "Then it really wasn't him who caused her illness. I wish I knew what it was . . . It's a terrifying thing to watch."

"Yes."

"What have you found in the wood? I know it's early yet, but you were most likely out there before the snow finished melting. Myrtle blooms early, and violet; I could use both."

"I haven't—" I cleared my throat. "I haven't been out there yet."

His brows flickered; I had astonished him. "Have you been ill, Rois?"

"No. I've just been busy, with Laurel . . ." I paused, felt his clear, practiced gaze. I asked, without meeting it, "Did anyone ever find Corbet? Or hear any news of him?"

"No." He set a stopper in the jar mouth and reached for his seal. He said, melting wax, "Corbet Lynn has passed from gossip into one of the village mysteries, along with the stranger at his hearth, and whose baby it really was that got left at Ley Gett's door that summer . . ."

"No one came looking for the stranger?"

"I've kept him on ice, waiting for someone to claim him. But I can't leave him there much longer in this weather. It's time to put him under. I don't know what else to do with him."

I thought of Tearle, the outcast of two worlds, trapped in one even after death, about to be given a stranger's grave in the other. "Let me see him," I begged without thinking: His face was all I had of Corbet. I felt Blane's surprise, raised my eyes to meet his sudden suspicion. I added lamely, "I feel sorry for him. He died so young in a place where no one knows him."

"Rois—"

"There's nothing more I can tell you. But he can't just go into his grave without anyone sparing him a thought. He died beside me; I may have been asleep, but at least he wasn't entirely alone. I suppose you could say that of anyone around here, I knew him best."

"I suppose you could say that." I heard other things in Blane's even voice, questions that he would have to take to his own grave, because I would never answer them. He turned; I followed him through the inner room, and out the back door into sunlight. The stone icehouse, big enough to hold a coffin or two, windowless and with only one door, looked as likely a vault as any. "Best stay outside a moment," Blane suggested as he unlatched the door. "He's surrounded by ice and stone, but sometimes, when the weather changes, things get in . . ."

He stood there in the doorway without moving, without speaking, for a long time, letting the place air out, I thought, while I watched some birds fly north over Ley Gett in his field furrowing south. Then I looked at the apothecary's back. Still he hadn't moved; he might have been turned to stone.

"What is it?"

He didn't hear me. I went to the door finally and saw what he saw in the clear spring light.

The man lying there had long grey hair and a strong, aged face marked with all the lines and shadows of one who had travelled his way through human time. I recognized him; a ghost of his beauty lingered, in the graceful bones of cheek and jaw, in his hands. Tears of wonder stung my eyes: He was no longer spellbound. She could not hold him, or she no longer wanted him; she had relinquished him to time.

I didn't know I had stopped breathing until I took a breath again. "If you ask the oldest in the village," I said shakily, "they'll probably tell you who he is."

"I'm sure they will." I had never heard Blane's voice so dry. "And I'm sure you won't." I said nothing. He closed the door gently, so not to wake the dead. "The stranger we found in Lynn Hall died of natural causes, and I'll swear that on my father's bones to anyone who asks. Whatever haunted Lynn Hall has exacted its price. Enough is enough. I'll bury him tonight in an unnamed grave. If he's still around."

I heard Nial Lynn's voice out of the past: *No one will know you when you die . . . Even your gravestone will stand silent* . . . My skin prickled. They had all been true, as Corbet said, all the curses. Except that I had known Tearle, I had seen . . . I had changed that curse at least, in spite of Nial Lynn; his son's unmarked stone would speak its tale to me.

I left Tearle Lynn at least in peace, but I still couldn't bring myself to go back to the wood. It seemed a shadow world I was afraid to return to, even in memory—not alone, not without Corbet. And I didn't know if I would ever see him again, outside of the dream where I had left him. Maybe, I thought, that's where he had always been. So my dream had told me in the end.

And then one morning I opened my window to the soft air, and heard the familiar sound of hammering from within the wood.

I stared, stunned, across the sunlit green. I thought of Laurel, and my throat closed. I whirled, not knowing what to do, and bumped into her as she came in to find me.

She held my shoulders. "It's all right, Rois. I knew he was back."

"When—?How—?" I could not speak. He had not come to find me; I might not know this stranger who had returned to Lynn Hall. Everything had happened; maybe nothing had happened. A man rebuilding his house had gone away in winter and returned in spring.

"He sent me a letter. He asked Salish to give it to our father. He read it and gave it to me. He—"

"When?"

"A few days ago. He must have gotten people to work for him again. Salish said all those wild stories about him came down to nothing but a stranger falling ill during a storm and wandering into Lynn Hall." She paused, the faint, anxious line appearing between her brows. "Rois—you're not still—"

"No." I shook my head quickly. "No." That seemed a lie, but so did "yes"; I did not know in what dream I might still love him. "I'm just startled. Go on."

"So was I. I wanted time to think—that's why I didn't tell you. Then I realized that there wasn't very much left of anything to think about."

"What did he say?"

"That he had had to leave unexpectedly in the middle of that storm. There were urgent family matters. And then someone died. He had no time to send a message. Later, he began to realize that he might never be able to come back, and there seemed no way to tell me that. That's what he wrote. I'm not sure what he meant. He could not find a way to return here until winter's end. He said that he hoped some day I would forgive his silence, as well as any trouble he had caused. He said he understood that might not be easy."

"Have you?"

"What?"

"Forgiven him?"

She was silent a little; I watched the blood rise in her face. She smiled the dancing, sunlit smile she teased Perrin with, and I hugged her suddenly.

"You're going to marry Perrin."

"He found a way to forgive me."

"And Corbet?"

"I don't seem to have room to remember being hurt," she answered simply. "He said that if I ever wanted to see him as a friend, I should write to him, but that he wouldn't come here without permission. I'm glad you're not angry with me, Rois."

"For what?"

"For not listening to you. For causing you and Perrin and our father so much grief. You were right all the time. I should have waited for spring."

I waited, watching the green deepen in the wood, the sodden fields turn tidy with straight furrows, the first faint color wash along them. I was afraid of his politeness, his indifference, I knew, so I waited until I could bear it, if he had nothing more than that to give me.

I went one morning when Laurel had gone on her first ride to the village, and our father was in the fields, and there was no one to ask where I went. I started briskly, with one thing on my mind. But as I rode into the wood it showed me a hundred things to catch my attention: hyacinths and wood anemones, great pink and gold raspberry blossoms, hawthorn, lacy dogwood, lady's-slipper, purple trillium. It lured me here and there, it spoke my name in small white blossoms. I rode past all its distractions, for every fall of the hammer on Lynn Hall drove a name deeper into my heart, and the closer I came to it, the harder my own heart pounded. Remember this, the wood said. Remember that. There seemed nothing I could forget, and no peace or mercy in remembering.

He saw me from among the peaked, raw beams rising on his roof. Crispin, working with him, stopped pounding nails a moment to wave at me. But Corbet dropped his hammer and went to the ladder. I slid off my horse, clung to her, suddenly terrified. I could not look a man in the eyes and ask him if, in any world, he had ever turned into ivy. If he had lived among his own ghosts. If he had ever loved me or if I had only dreamed that he had. If he had ever been real in my eyes at all, and if not, then what polite stranger had spoken my name all winter.

"Rois."

I forced myself to look at him. He wore a homespun work shirt, rolled at the elbows, loose at the neck; I saw the sweat glisten in the hollow of his throat. His eyes seemed stranger's eyes, full of light that now hid nothing: the faint shadow of trouble in them, the brief indecision before he spoke again.

"Thank you for coming. I hoped—somehow—you would not be too angry with me."

"No." Words stuck. I had to clear my throat, pick through them carefully, to find the words that belonged only in this world. I could feel my hands trembling; I wound the reins tightly through my fingers. "Laurel told me you had written to her. You vanished so suddenly. We thought—we didn't know—" I faltered under his unfamiliar gaze. "We thought everything. Even that you might have died."

"It was cruel of me," he said simply, "to leave like that."

"It seemed cruel." I unwound my hands, feeling my way a little more easily into memory, since I knew we both remembered that at least. "Laurel said you had some urgent family matters."

He nodded. "I was called home. And then my father died."

I blinked. Worlds merged briefly, separated. "I'm sorry—"

"It was quite unexpected. But I found myself tangled in family affairs for so long, I was afraid I might not make it back here."

"You were afraid?"

He smiled a little, then. "Winter didn't frighten me away. I did want to return." He paused, studying me a moment. "You look well. But changed. Was the winter hard?"

"Yes. Very."

"How is your father? And Laurel?"

"They're both well." I watched his eyes. "Laurel is going to be married soon, to Perrin."

I saw little in his eyes but relief. "I'm glad," he said softly; like Laurel's memories, his had not survived the winter storms. "That's the way it should be. Is she happy?" He read the answer in my face; the tension left his own. "I'm glad," he said again.

There seemed suddenly nothing left to say; only Crispin's hammer spoke. Words turned back into dreams; they would fade eventually, I knew. Eventually. I shifted awkwardly, wondering how to say goodbye, wondering if there had been any world in which we did not.

"Well—"

"I know," he said abruptly, "why you seem so changed. You didn't walk barefoot through my wood. You rode here, and you're wearing shoes."

I glanced down at them, surprised. I found him seeing other things in me, an expression in my eyes, maybe, or something I had done to my hair. "You seem changed, too," I said. "Winter was hard on us all."

"Yes." He drew a deep breath of the tantalizing air then, and his face opened as he turned to contemplate his house. "I think this time it will be different," he said, more to himself than to me. I did not ask him what he meant.

"I should go. No one knows where I am."

"You never worried about that before," he commented. It made me smile, that he remembered. His answering smile, brief but warm, seemed unfamiliar, too. "There is something that I wanted to ask you, Rois. That is, if you found your way to speaking to me again."

"What?" I asked vaguely, hearing only my name again, his voice saying it.

"About my garden. Or what passes for it. Oh—and something else." He reached into his shirt pocket. "Before I forget. I found this in my house. I wonder if you know who it belongs to."

I looked at what lay on his palm. Then I looked at him. I closed my eyes suddenly, feeling light like gold on my mouth, seeing gold behind my eyes. All the words I knew freed themselves again, to visions, dreams, her wild wood, my wood.

"Rois?" He touched me lightly. I opened my eyes.

"Yes." I wanted to weep, I wanted to laugh, as I took my mother's ring from him. "I know whose it is." I slipped it into my skirt pocket; this time it would not turn into leaves. I met his eyes, filled my eyes with him, looking for all the small things I had loved. I found them still there. I could reach out to them or not; he could say yes, he could say no. He smiled at me suddenly, not understanding what he saw, but drawn to it. Freedom, I could have told him: a new word for both of us.

"What was the other thing you wanted to ask? About your garden?"

"Oh. The old rose trees. Some are still alive, I think. But so wild and overgrown with ivy I don't know if they'll bloom. I wondered if you might look at them."

"They survived the winter?"

"Even that winter."

I looked beyond him to the garden, where the buttermilk mare cropped placidly in a patch of grass.

"Rois? Do you think you might?"

Beyond the garden the young leaves on the trees had turned the wood a misty green. Shadows lay within the mist, and unexpected falls of light, the mysteries of its seasons, ancient, familiar, forever unpredictable.

"I might," I said. "Yes."